Felicity McLean's debut novel, *The Van Apfel Girls are Gone*, has been published in more than half a dozen countries. It was a Barnes & Noble Discover Great New Writers pick in the US, and was shortlisted for the Indie Book Awards and longlisted for the UK's Dagger Awards and the Davitt.

Her book *Body Lengths*, co-written with Olympian Leisel Jones, was Apple Books Best Biography of 2015 and won the 2016 Australian Book Industry Awards People's Choice for Small Publisher Adult Book of the Year.

RED

FELICITY McLEAN

FOURTH ESTATE

Fourth Estate
An imprint of HarperCollins*Publishers*

HarperCollins*Publishers*
Australia • Brazil • Canada • France • Germany • Holland • India
Italy • Japan • Mexico • New Zealand • Poland • Spain • Sweden
Switzerland • United Kingdom • United States of America

First published in Australia in 2022
by HarperCollins*Publishers* Australia Pty Limited
Level 13, 201 Elizabeth Street, Sydney NSW 2000
ABN 36 009 913 517
harpercollins.com.au

A catalogue record for this book is available from the National Library of Australia

ISBN 978 1 4607 5509 9 (paperback)
ISBN 978 1 4607 0944 3 (ebook)
ISBN 978 1 4607 4259 4 (audiobook)

Cover design by Darren Holt, HarperCollins Design Studio
Cover image © Georgii Cherniadev/Trevillion Image
Author photograph by A.Hollingworth/HiredGun
Typeset in Bembo Std by Kelli Lonergan
Printed and bound in Australia by McPherson's Printing Group

MIX
Paper from responsible sources
FSC www.fsc.org FSC® C001695

For Dad

What follows is a fictionalised version of the Central Coast of New South Wales. Details have been invented. Geographies altered. Liberties have been taken.

FIRST OFF

Sid had promised that Datsun was gold to be honest it wasn't even bronze but what did I care I must've only been four or five years old the day we collected Sid's car from Wyoming and drove it the long way home just the two of us Sid and me in the full dazzle of summer sun and the whole time Sid's singing 'Hi-Yo Silver' though that Datsun's supposedly gold yeah we drove home in the sunshine singing 'Hi-Yo Silver' it's the earliest memory of my dad that I've got.

Sid let me ride shotgun probably even called it that in that daggy way he used to say *howdy pardner* and *saddle up* and *you ride shotgun* even though I didn't know what a shotgun was wouldn't have known one if it bit me on the bum I still don't if you want to know the truth yeah despite what they say about me.

And so what if Sid let me ride in the front passenger seat sure there were probably laws against that kind of thing but still there's me sitting up next to him yeah perched like royalty on his balled-up jacket just so's I could see over the dash. And through the windscreen on the bonnet the sun's yolk sat fair and square like the whole world was served up for us.

That Datsun was a two-tone white-brown number like riding round in a block of Cadbury's Top Deck. Yeah the 180B was Sid's first car and they say you never forget your first sure there were other cars before the Datsun and there've been other cars since like the Sandman that Sid was just minding for a mate and later the Torana that showed up and then shot through so quick it gave a kid whiplash to witness but that Datsun was the first car that Sid paid good money for probably the only one if I'm honest with you and who cares that it was used and that it came with used cigarette smoke and burns on the bucket seats to boot because that Datsun was ours it was mine and Sidney's.

Sid was tickled pink with the sh█t-coloured thing.

—

And as we drove home that day Sid sang that's right he was hi-yo-silvering his mangy heart out and ignoring the fact the car wasn't silver and not even copper no truly it wasn't metallic. Coast air rushed in through the open windows and the Datsun cantered along and the song of that drive was whirring tyres and whistling wind yeah that plus the strains of Sid's song.

But just as Sid got to the hi-yo-silvery part yeah as soon as he hit the bit that I knew up came the cops behind us blue lights flashing high beams blinking and their siren drowning out Sidney's tune. They directed us to pull over so Sid slipped off the highway and into an emergency bay and we sat silent in that shoulder of the Pacific Highway yeah waiting to learn our offence.

And didn't the cops take their own sweet time getting out of their patrol car that day. I guess even at that age I must've asked Sid what we'd done wrong but if he answered I don't remember his reply. Fear had swooped in and stolen Sid's voice or maybe it was anger hard to say.

I remember those cops though there were two of them there at Sid's windowsill all swagger and smirk yeah all scorn. Asking to see Sid's licence and is this you Mr McCoy as if Sid might be anyone else and where did you get this vehicle Mr McCoy and can we see your rego papers Mr McCoy we need to make sure everything's in order Mr McCoy ensure you're the rightful owner you know make sure you're the real McCoy as if they were the first ones to joke about our name yeah like they invented that gag.

They were probably only young probably just sh█t-kicking junior officers but when you're not old enough to see over the dash without a cushion everyone seems like a monster especially if they're in a uniform. One of them was skinny while the other was giant he looked like he should of come with his own moons seriously you'd of thought they were cartoon cops if you didn't know how dangerous those pigs could be.

The skinny one had a high-pitched voice and an Adam's apple that wobbled in his throat when he talked he leaned on the windowsill of Sid's new Datsun and pushed his face so far into the car that Sid had to recoil or risk getting pig spit all over himself. The big one stood behind him and glanced around from time to time I don't know if he was supposed to be standing guard or what but the way his gut oozed over his belt he would've had a battle on his hands if he needed to access his holster in a hurry yeah hardly what you'd call Quick Draw McGraw.

Outchagetmate the skinny one said his voice dripping with false reluctance like he hated the position that Sid put him in oh he hated to have to do it.

Stay put Red Sid instructed.

And I knew he meant business because he'd gone and called me Red. Red meant listen here kiddo Red meant *now*. Red was what Sid said when he wasn't mucking around if he called me Ruby I'd pretend I hadn't heard.

Because you can give a kid a name but you cannot make her drink Sid undid his seatbelt warily. He went to open the door but the skinny cop refused to move so now their foreheads were almost touching and Sid was forced to ask permission just to open his own door it's the small injustices that burn the worst. And I might've only been small myself my sandals barely scraped the plastic mats but already I hated those cops with a vengeance my five-year-old fury stretched sky-high.

Out of the car Sid stood as directed facing the Datsun his legs parted his arms spread wide his palms were raised to the sky it was a blisteringly hot day yeah early December must've been thirty-eight in the shade. And I can't relay their exact conversation it were like a decade or so ago but trust me when I say those cops they were feeling loquacious that day Sid barely said a word it's hard to believe I know but the pigs did all the talking you can take it from me.

Then those dogs they made Sid press against the car door he was head and shoulders above the metal roof heat radiated off it. I could see his square of lemon shirt at the window two dark patches blossoming under each short sleeve silence then a dull thud when his cheek was forced down on the roof.

—

When Sid got back in the car afterwards he'd left part of himself behind. Sure he was a gangly motherf█er yeah Sid had plenty of length to spare. But before the cops pulled us over he drove with his head cocked sideways to stop it touching the car-roof lining but now as he sat back down in the driver's seat Sid was shorter than when he'd got out. Somehow he fitted easily his shoulders drooped and his mouth did too yeah something inside his chest had shrivelled Sid lost actual centimetres that day he got stopped by the cops he left them on the F3 southbound I swear.

His cheek was red where it'd kissed the car roof a blotch stretched from his eye socket to his jaw as if the blood was simmering too close to the surface blood boiling or more likely shame. Sid never said if they charged him with anything who knows maybe they got him for having a kid in the front passenger seat I've heard worse but charging us wasn't the point no the point was to make our lives a misery as if that might make up for theirs.

And so it goes day in and day out and no time and a half on Sundays yeah there's no rest for the wicked no rest from their Sisyphean mission. What I know all about Sisyphus just like I know about those cops oh they bully us into submission and so we say nothing and so the cops bully us again. And when those cops drove past the car yard in Wyoming that day and saw Sid chewing the fat with the dealer well then they simply waited yeah they waited until we were driving away in Sid's spanking-new-but-really-second-hand rolled-gold beige-tainted Datsun and then those bastards tailed us.

And then having rattled old Sid like they did they went and left us in the midday sun in the lay-by on the side of the road. There was no sound no 'Hi-Yo Silver' from Sid no nothing only the sad seagull squeal of metal against metal as that fat cop keyed the side of Sid's car as they sauntered away.

—

Everyone knows how it ends what people are less interested in hearing is how it all got started. Nobody cares that we never asked for it that we never asked for *anything* let alone trouble we didn't put up our hands for police persecution but we received it all the same.

And the newspapers they never mention the fact that my mum died when I was only three weeks old that she bled out as a result of complications from my birth the kind of complications that don't occur in the rich yeah they strictly afflict those on the dole.

And even though she died in the main street where she was picking up something for a friend you get the feeling that no local councillor or funds manager no f■■■ing court judge rushed over to help her yeah bet their kind never haemorrhage to death ahead of the lunchtime rush in the middle of Mann Street Plaza.

So that's the first hole in the story a glaring blank space like a censorship mark a hole where my mum should have been but nobody takes that hole into account when they're telling my story for me.

—

I had Sid of course and he was hardly a hole you could accuse Sid of heaps and plenty of people did but you couldn't level that particular crime at him. My dad was the opposite of a hole he was a long lean beanpole of a thing full of life full of beans a skinny streak of kinetic energy who could drive a tinny or fix a fence or fell a tree or pick a lock but who had to physically sit on his hands in order to keep them still.

Sid's family were from this place so he grew up knowing the Central Coast like the back of his quick-fingered hand. He knew to wet his line at Juno Point for jewfish and Forresters for whiting while your best bet for black bream was the low ledge down there at Terrigal. He knew that Soldiers and Shelly and Putty and Killcare consistently turned on a feed. He knew Davistown was the go for pipis and Bateaux Bay for blue gropers and Veteran Hall Wharf was a sure thing for flatties or leather jackets. He knew that prawns ran in the months with an 'r' in the name (but somehow still came home bucket-empty during September through to April). Way back when he knew how to get served at the Royal Hotel when you were still too young to have hairs on your balls and where to climb the fence into the Erina drive-in any night of the week. He knew how to get into the Avoca Beach flicks without a ticket to watch the

Saturday matinee but don't try it on a Sunday because that's when they held Catholic mass in the theatre let me tell you Sid only made that mistake once. Yeah Sid reckoned he knew just about everything that was worth knowing about the place this stretch of coast shaped Sid it made him who he was Sid was of this place and he was *because* of this place yeah geography can really shape a person so if you're going to try to lay the blame square on Sid's shoulders I'm sorry but maybe take a look around first.

Sid used to say they'd have to carry him out in a box he warned you he wouldn't go willingly the problem was neither would Sergeant Healy he was stuck to this place just as much as Sid was. Two barnacles on the same pissy rock. Not that you'd know it from the public record mind you the sergeant's role barely rates a mention his name rarely crops up in the court transcripts you never hear about Sergeant Healy's sins on the nightly news but that's an oversight of the highest order yeah that's a mistake right there his role is hardly marginal hardly what you'd call immaterial and for the court not to hear about it is to have a great gaping hole in proceedings big enough to drive a road train through yeah it's because of him that I'm in here.

—

Our first offence was being too smart for those Healys let me tell you something for nothing yeah I'll give you this for free: dumb ████ like the Healys hate being reminded how stupid they are especially by plebs like us it was Sid's dad – my grandad – that got the ball rolling. Sid's dad was made in the same mould as Sid or more accurately the other way around yeah they say my grandad was as fidgety as Sid. He was slower of course by the time I knew him he was pushing sixty when I was born but we still called him Pep instead of Pop yeah that man was perpetual motion.

Pep's people came from Broke if you really want to know. That's northwest of here more than an hour away by car and longer if that car's a Datsun. And so there's Pep sitting in class one day keeping his head down when the school inspector arrived he decided to teach an impromptu lesson. Why do we learn history the school inspector wanted to know but nobody in Pep's class could tell him. Alright the school inspector said I'll tell you we learn history so we're not doomed to repeat the mistakes of the past and Pep liked that yeah he was taken with that answer so he wrote the school inspector's words down on the inside back cover of his book you know for a rainy day.

You won't believe it but two weeks later Pep's family they left Broke to move closer to the coast and they settled in a white weatherboard house in Wyoming and honestly I'm not making this up but in Pep's first week at his new school who should walk in but the school inspector he was there to teach an impromptu lesson. Why do we learn history the school inspector wanted to know and the boys stared out the window yeah they watched the peewees perched on the playground fence and counted divots in the cricket pitch until finally Pep took pity and he opened up his workbook and he read out loud what he'd written in the inside back cover just over a fortnight before – so we're not doomed to repeat the mistakes of the past.

Didn't the school inspector look like a stunned mullet yeah like he'd been slapped in the mouth with a wet fish.

Get yourself down to the school office son and wait for me there oh he was massively impressed with Pep. And when he'd finished teaching the rest of the class (who were doomed to thirty-five more minutes of history with the school inspector) then he went down to the school office himself and there he informed Pep that he was a bright kid yeah a bright kid with a bright future and that Wyoming State School was no place for a kid like Pep and he was transferring Pep to a school in the city. So now it was Pep's turn to look like a stunned mullet his family had only just moved to Wyoming yeah here was Pep in spitting distance of the ocean for the first time in his life and the school inspector wanted to send him away? Pep didn't think so.

But when Pep explained all this to the school inspector how he'd only just moved to Wyoming yeah from Broke and how with respect the school inspector had taught the exact same lesson only a fortnight ago in Broke and how Pep had copied down the school inspector's answer word-for-verbatim yeah it wasn't like he came up with it himself but that only made things worse.

A kid who wanted to learn and who recognised top-shelf teaching when he saw it? The school inspector's mind was made up and Pep's fate was sealed and so you see how we've always lived according to the whims of the powerful and Pep was shipped off to school in Sydney the same week he never got to live in the white weatherboard in Wyoming worse he was separated from his family.

But if you think that's the end of Pep's problems well saddle up and settle back as Sid always says because Pep's strife was just getting started.

You see Sergeant Healy's old man Howard was also in class the day the school inspector arrived and it was a visit that Howard Healy had anticipated yeah he'd spent months waiting for the school inspector to show up. Howard Healy had big plans he had his eye on a career in the law starting with a superior education down in the city. That's right he was getting the hell out of Wyoming he was going to finish his schooling in Sydney before progressing to some degree at a sandstone university before being admitted as a lawyer and passing the bar and making partner and becoming a flipping courtroom judge how the hell should I know. All I know is that Sid said that Pep said that Healy Senior talked about his law career like it was f█ing preordained like he may as well of received his degree already that's how supremely sure of himself he was yeah Howard Healy had so many tickets on himself he could of run a chook raffle he was so far up his arse he could see out his own mouth. But what he hadn't anticipated was Pep arriving at school and stealing his future out from under his stuck-up f█ing nose no Howard Healy hadn't banked on that. He hadn't banked on us McCoys yeah Pep's intelligence was his curse oh it was our whole family's curse.

—

And maybe it would of been alright if it ended there with Pep going off to school in the city and that. But as soon as Pep had done his time in Sydney he got on the first train back to

Wyoming where he was turned around at Narara station and sent back to Sydney it was World War II and Pep was given his marching orders. That's right Pep was conscripted into the Australian Military Forces having just spent all those years filling his head with education now they wanted him to get it blown off he served in Sydney for two years until he was told in 1944 he was being sent to fight the Japanese in New Guinea. Pep had no beef with the Japanese he had no beef with anybody much and he sure as hell didn't want to fire a rifle so he found himself a frock yeah Pep became Bernice they never thought to give Bernice a gun.

What you're telling me you wouldn't do the same? Be a better world if there was less war and more cross-dressing but the military authorities didn't see it that way no they hold a different view. They call people like Pep deserters and criminals they call you an unpatriotic dog Pep was discharged in absentia for misconduct because of illegal absence.

That was our family's first run-in with the law and all because Pep was averse to killing and murdering that's right look out for us wild McCoys watch out for us pacifists with our dangerous peace-loving ways it wasn't until 1948 that an amnesty for deserters was declared and Pep was pardoned or whatever they call it but the damage had been done. Yeah God help a man who refuses to be an ANZAC and doubly if he does it in a dress.

What a threat Pep must've been to the authorities back then what with him all unarmed and them with their Glock pistols and their batons no wonder when they worked out what he was up to they were forced to beat him so badly he was hospitalised for a month yeah no choice but to assault him like they did.

Sure Pep might've avoided violence in the jungles of New Guinea he might've dodged the bullet that was Bougainville but Pep saw his fair share of hate and hostility yeah Pep saw the wrong end of plenty of bloodied batons without laying eyes on the enemy.

And who knows maybe it was this trauma Pep passed on to Sid the sort of shellshock that comes without needing to see a single shell. The kind of pain that comes cloaked in a pink floral frock no wonder why we dislike the law.

When Pep got back to Wyoming after his stint as Bernice he was quieter slower than when he went. Had the pep beaten right out of him the family reckoned but you'd better believe Howard Healy was on hand to welcome Pep home to Wyoming. Fresh from the frontline in Milne Bay still wearing his military boots Howard Healy knew just how you treated deserters and so everything Pep suffered in the city he suffered all over again in Wyoming thanks to Howard Healy talk about being doomed to repeat the mistakes of the past.

So you see it was personal from the start this whole saga was personal the Healys' grievances were personal and their hatred for our family was f■■ing personal but don't kid yourself for one second that that's all it was no it was so much more than that. What you think the Healys hated the McCoys for three generations because Pep knew the right answer in class you think all those years of harassment all that brutality was just because Pep stayed home from the war. No the fact is those Healys are fixers they're corrupt as they come bent as your toilet U-bend and filthy as too. When he couldn't be a lawyer (because of the war because of a thousand things but not all because of Pep) well then Howard Healy became a cop a disillusioned one who trained his son the same way. Taking bribes falsifying documents roughing up witnesses bashing suspects removing evidence planting evidence arresting without charge diverting internal investigations nothing was too much trouble no nothing was ever off limits and sure they'd say theirs are so-called victimless crimes but all that means is: in their eyes the victims don't count.

The McCoys and the Healys were never equals in the eyes of the law and by the eyes of the law I mean that dumb ███ Sergeant Healy. The Healys hated us for what Pep had done and also for what he hadn't but more than that they hated us for what we represented yeah they looked down on us like a floater in a public pool. To the Healys we were dole bludgers we were housos we were blue-collar union scum we were durry smokers bong users we were poor. We were everything the Healys of this world despised and it didn't matter that Sid and I weren't even half these things and that we were law abiding for the most part we hadn't committed any real offence until the cops goaded us into it and by that stage they'd left us no choice. But that didn't matter not to Sergeant Healy and not to his pig mates all that mattered was that it was started bet they never thought it'd be finished by me.

—

It wasn't always that way Sid and I lived happily enough in the early years the Datsun Years I like to think of them as because that's when they start in my memory around the time we first drove that Datsun 180B home those years were more golden than anything on earth more golden than Sid's car ever was.

We lived in a weatherboard house that must've been white once upon a time only our house had turned a dirty grey with age and with the breeze that blew in off the bay.

Our place was halfway up a hill overlooking Brisbane Water and being halfway up a hill meant you could stand in the front yard with its besser-block letterbox and its gnome fishing optimistically in a dry concrete pond and depending on which direction you faced you could look out over the sparkling expanse of the bay or you could cop an eyeful of uphill road.

Then if you walked down the hill towards the bay your Achilles shrinking your toes gripping the rubber of your thongs then you arrived at an enormous sprawling angophora that split the road like a peach. That tree was so huge and so ancient that even the council knew when they were beaten and rather than remove it they simply rerouted the road so it flowed around both sides of the tree and you could pick the tourists easy enough they were the ones who baulked at the fork like there was an actual choice to be made. But the rest of us knew that both roads rejoined on the far side of the tree and also that things swung sharply to the left yeah you didn't want to take that last bend too efficiently it was pull up or end up in the bay.

—

Sid taught me to ride a bike on that hill my lungs bursting my hair streaming too terrified to scream or brake or do anything but ride. A kid became a fast learner on Jabiru Avenue that's for sure yeah gifted and talented in the face of that gradient and all without a Stackhat or training wheels and definitely without Spokey Dokeys tinkling on my spokes like other kids had but on the other hand I had Sid on the sidelines cheering like a maniac he had a heart like Phar Lap Sid did yeah he barracked each time I sat in the saddle he cheered like it was the Tour de flipping France.

—

Jabiru Avenue was where Sid taught me to go crabbing too there at the bottom of the hill in the gentle belly of the bay we'd go looking for mud crabs or blue swimmers though we never spied many of the latter and not enough of the former for my liking either.

The problem was Sid and his bleeding heart.

It didn't matter how many hoops or nets or pots or lines we lugged down that hill or how many gangs I threaded with bait we always walked home with an empty bucket swinging there between us and me with a face like a dropped pie. Every crab was too small or too big or too blue or too wet no Sid never saw a crab we could keep. Taste better from the shop anyway he'd console himself as if the crabs beached on ice in the takeaway shop hadn't once been swimming around some bay until someone else scooped them out but then Sid never liked being the one to do the dirty deed.

Sid taught me other things too not just how to ride a bike and catch a crab or not catch a crab as the case may be. He taught me that family means something and loyalty means everything yeah he taught me to be a girl of my word. But they were the Datsun Years so golden now in my memory and that's the third hole in this story that you've been fed. A great whopping omission just like all the other lies. This is the hole that says of course we were always going to turn out this way us McCoys we were destined for a sticky end. This is the hole that says beginning is ending that says origin is fate this is the hole that says what we suffered was what we deserved. Yeah we had it coming all along this hole says we were rotten from the start.

Because as soon as you tell the part of the story where we were happy yeah as soon as you say that Sid and I were getting along just fine until Sergeant Healy and the New South Wales Police Service came along then that's when you're forced to admit that the fault doesn't lie with us no my life wasn't always going to end up this way.

But that's us now isn't it the (un)holy McCoys more sinning than saintly but shot through with holes or more specifically: our story is.

That thing is chock-full of holes the way the courts and the media tell it *petchoo petchoo petchoo* count them. *Petchoo* a hole for where my mum should have been. *Petchoo* a hole where Sergeant Healy's role in all this is never mentioned. *Petchoo petchoo petchoo* that great whacking hole of preordainment that gets the New South Wales Police Service off the hook. Our story as it stands is chock-full of holes any idiot can tell you history's written by the victors yeah whoever wields the power wields the biro.

—

But I'm not dead yet no I'm not going quietly I'm here to set the record straight while I can yeah I'm here to fill in a few gaps in my story here to plug a few holes don't you know.

—

The kind of child who probably burned ants with a magnifying glass that's how one newspaper described me. I never burned any ants with a magnifying glass and not with anything else either but for the record I could burn through a person with a single stare yeah just so that you're aware.

—

It wasn't just my stare that got me in trouble at school my mouth helped too and sometimes my fists if it came to that though most teachers got sick of my mouth long before they had a chance to get fed up with my fists.

Why don't you come up here and teach the class if you think you can do a better job they'd say and I wouldn't skip a beat.

Miss teaching's a unionised workforce I'd say. What you want me to go around stealing union jobs have some honour why would you joke about that.

—

Things I've been dared to eat (and did):

> chewed gum from the floor of the B55 bus to Ettalong Beach
> copper-sulphate crystals from the chemistry storeroom
> seventeen potato scallops from the fish-and-chips shop (a record)
> a cold cigarette stub
> a warm Band-Aid
> a Year Eight maths test torn into two-centimetre squares each time the teacher turned to face the blackboard
> the gherkins from nine McDonald's Junior Burgers after they were flung at the ceiling and fell to the floor and were scooped up and put in my burger
> a fistful of potting mix
> a litre of orange cordial *undiluted*
> a litre of red cordial *undiluted*
> a dollar coin but I never swallowed that only stuck it in my mouth for a bit because seriously who can stomach Her Maj also what a waste of a buck.

Yeah I might've walked away from a fight or three but I never backed down from a dare.

—

When I was little my neighbours' pet rabbit escaped from its hutch and got loose in the street where it was run over by a car. Back in those days I used to climb the fence into the Moffatts' backyard and pat that rabbit during the daytime when the Moffatts weren't home I cried for two days when it died.

Chin up Ruby Tuesday Sid said. Flat rabbit still makes a good stew.

And Sid maintains my reply isn't fit to be printed who knew the filth that could come out of a little kid's mouth.

That's when I told him I was running away.

And Sid said he'd miss me but I was probably old enough to make my own way in the world especially if I didn't have a sense of humour yeah there was no need to get all vegetarian about it.

All what.

All vegetarian. Someone who turns their nose up at perfectly good food and they get skinnier and skinnier until there's no meat left on their bones.

Which was a bit rich when you think about it yeah coming from him who couldn't catch crabs.

So I packed my pjs and my nightlight and an orange in a cardboard box I dragged it halfway down Jabiru Avenue then I sat beside my box and I ate my orange and watched the sun setting over the bay while I tried to figure out if I was too stubborn to turn around and go home. This took some figuring and the light was fading and I must've got scared or bored or honestly who knows what was going on inside my tiny brain because I climbed inside that box in the middle of the road and pulled the cardboard flaps closed over my head.

And that's where I was when Warren Kenny rumbled over the crest of the hill with one hand gripping a half-smoked cigarette and the other gripping the steering wheel of his Mack Granite. Warren Kenny used to ferry sandstone around the quarry at Somersby in the days before he got laid off but after that the Mack Granite tray was always empty and come to think of it so was Warren Kenny.

But on this day Warren wasn't empty on this day Warren had stopped off at the White Hart for a schooner or six and so he thought he was seeing things when he spied my brown box sitting there in the middle of Jabiru Avenue. He'd slipped that Mack Granite down into second gear by the time he realised what he was seeing: a cardboard box probably empty or maybe full of old newspapers either way it would make a satisfying pop when it burst underneath 110 tonnes of Mack Granite. Warren Kenny squared up my box with his tyre line and shifted down to first to let the jake brake do its job when by some fluke some flip of the coin Warren Kenny changed his mind at the last minute he swerved to the left and he drove on past my cardboard box and my head popped up and my curls bobbed about in that Mack Granite rear-view mirror and Warren Kenny almost had a heart attack.

Nearly flattened her. Nearly bloody flattened her he said to Sid afterwards. Jesus I nearly spread her all over the road.

Warren was sucking so hard on his cigarette that thing was in danger of being digested.

Jesus Christ he said again. I could've made mincemeat out of her Sid.

Could not I said hotly I had my box tucked awkwardly under one arm. I'm a vegetarian Warren Kenny there's no meat on *my* bones.

She's a handful Sid admitted to Warren. Two handfuls actually.

—

Two handfuls and no bones about it.

—

Me: You ever wish I was a son?

Sid: You ever wish I was a mum?

Me: Already got one of those thanks she might be dead but she's still my mum you know.

Sid: Yeah well I've got a son too so we're even.

Me: Wait what —

Sid: Scott's his name.

Me: —

Sid: It's about time you found out.

Me: —

Sid: Was always going to tell you one day.

Me: —

Sid: Good man Scotty. He's got the hots for this chick called Charlene and she works in a garage and wears these lovely little brown overalls …

Me: —

Sid: Not sure if they're meant to be together or if they'll just end up as *neighbours* …

Me: *Siiiiid!*

Sid: Geddit? *Neighbours*. You know on the telly. Had you going for a while didn't I. Ah you can't beat an episode of *Neighbours*.

—

And he's laughing so hard he's at risk of splitting something yeah put a fork in Sid because he's done. But seriously I said didn't you ever want a son.

Not if this is how much trouble a daughter is he said and he cracked himself up again.

—

This is how much trouble a daughter is. No bones about it.

—

No bones about it but plenty of skeletons in the family closet. (Except in Pep's where there's no room for skeletons like you know because of the frocks.)

—

This one time Sid came to my high school it was careers day and Sid was showing us how to fillet a fish. Who cared if Sid wasn't a qualified chef or that his greatest culinary achievement was whisking the tablecloth out from under his beer without spilling a drop that one time. Because Sid claimed he had all the necessary tools to do the job yeah a fish and a knife. That was Sid.

And he bounced in wearing his Kiss the Chef apron. With his grin yeah his neon innocence.

Here was a classroom full of kids with piercings and peeling noses and lips covered in cold sores from hours spent in the surf and all the boys had those razor-toothed surfboard wax combs that doubled as beer-bottle openers poking out of their pockets and yeah there was Sid among all of this they were going to eat him alive.

I refused to watch while he did his demonstration didn't listen while he yabbered away but the rest of the class yeah they hung off each word couldn't they see he was making stuff up.

A female sunfish can lay ten million eggs per day he said.

Salmon can remember human faces.

Catfish have more tastebuds than dogs do.

Is that right said our teacher he was pale and washed out and he looked even more invisible next to Kiss-the-Chef Sid.

Then he said: I read that the clownfish can change gender. Is that true Mr McCoy?

Like Sid was *National Geographic* and not a chef (hell he wasn't even a chef but did that stop Sid).

Clownfish can change gender Sid repeated. Well sure and wouldn't you if you had the chance. You might finally know what your wife wanted.

He winked at our teacher.

So what I said loudly. That's nothing female Californian condors can reproduce without males.

And Sid grinned and he cleaned his filleting knife showily on the seat of his shorts.

Yeah he said. But where's the fun in that.

—

And I died then I actually left my own body Jesus Christ someone make him shut up.

You gunna be a chef like your old man everyone wanted to know oh they seriously believed that was his job.

No she's off to the university Sid answered for me.

Was I. University? That was news to me.

Still I can't say I hated the idea.

—

The story Sid likes to tell is that time I saved Stevie from drowning it was one of those pristine September mornings the sky prairie-empty. The bay was Smith's-chips original blue. Peewees peep-peeped placid in the mud the world was stippled sunshine and ripples and calm.

I walked along the mud flats where they boomeranged the bay there wasn't any rush to get to school you could almost smell the summer coming a kid could sniff it on the breeze my shoes were scuffed their soles made no imprints.

At school I loved learning loved reading I was such a dirty nerd but I wasn't so enamoured with the place that I was prepared to get beaten up for it down behind the bike racks because that's what happened if you got to school early yeah if you really had a brain you didn't arrive too enthusiastically before the bell but as I was rounding the curve of the bay there in half-half there between the glare and the shadow of the wharf I saw a splash at least I thought I did.

No quick flick of fin no nothing afterwards just a single salient plop a fish jumping or a bird bombing yeah a fish nothing fishier than that but then I saw a head emerge it was a human head it bobbed for a breath for less than a breath then it disappeared again someone was in the water by the wharf oh they were in it alright they were under the surface too long.

Conditions were not what you'd call dicey not by a long shot the bay could barely raise a ripple but a person could drown in two minutes if they hadn't been trained at the Sid School of Swim i.e. jump in and start paddling. I took off in the wrong direction my back to the bay I was headed for the steps of the jetty because I figured I was faster running along its wooden teeth than I was swimming out that first hundred metres.

I flung my shoes off my school bag was long gone the water slapped gently at the piers I scanned the surface nothing bobbed nothing floated whatever it had been was submarining now I started to think I'd dreamed it and then a splash something pale jerked was that an arm whatever it never even broke the glass.

I'm coming I shouted hang on I'm coming I didn't seriously think the poor bastard could hear me but you don't think do you – you just run and you run and you jump and then you fly and in that instant I was winged yeah transcendent I was avian then I plummeted and the cold was a punch in the guts. But oh I hauled myself to the surface and I backstroked breathed backstroked breathed head thumping mouth sucking in breath. I scanned the cloak of the water and the weird part was it was so beautiful I mean it was dazzlingly dizzyingly beautiful out there with the bay and the hills and the yachts past the point I remember thinking death shouldn't look as good as all this.

Then something walloped all the air out of me and another thing shoved my head under the next few seconds were jumbled and strange like trying to make sense of a spool of negatives where each photo's no cousin of the last. An arm then a foot then nothing but whitewash the thing thrashed and it clawed it was going five rounds with me and each time it did the blow forced me back also the tide gently ushered me away. I swam forward and swam forward I tried to get a grip on this kid tried to shove my arm under and wrap myself around his torso yeah to drag him onto his back and hold his mouth to the sky just like Sid'd taught me to do but the more I reached for him the more he pumped his arms kid was climbing an underwater ladder he flung his head back wildly almost cracked me in the jaw it was ridiculous he was going to drown on a tide that was flat as a tack.

And across the bay those yachts were the colour of whipped cream and all with those stupid names like *Don't Tell the Missus* and *She Got the House* yeah really hilarious stuff. Those boats sat slack in the sun like they might just dissolve one puff of wind and they'd evaporate.

In the end I drew myself up into a ball and I kicked him with the full force of my legs and in the instant that I winded him I was able to grab him round the waist I rolled him over and I yanked him to the surface. Stop it I ordered I had one arm across his chest I wedged it under his armpit and when I felt him go limp I knew he was taking in air I began the slow kick drag rest kick drag rest back to the wharf.

After a spew and a cry and some general carrying on I asked Stevie Madigan what the hell he was thinking why jump off the wharf when there's no one around to haul him out and when he swam like he wore concrete shoes.

I've got my bronze medallion he was indignant.

Your bronze medallion in what I said.

In swimming what else do you get a bronze medallion in.

I don't know sinking I suggested.

There were three Madigan brothers and Stevie was the youngest I'd see them sometimes walking to school and stuff his brothers were bigger than him but that wasn't saying much everyone was bigger than Stevie he was a runt.

Also there was a dog he said.

A dog.

Yeah a big dog right here on the wharf and he was having a go at me Stevie said. He was tied up to the post there but then he broke free and came after me he sure was ugly and mean even you would've jumped if you'd been here.

But I can swim.

He ignored me.

It was pretty quick thinking of me to jump into the water he said I would've been okay too if the current wasn't so strong.

We both turned and looked out over the bay where there wasn't a single white cap between here and the horizon below us pissy little waves lapped half-hearted against the piers honestly I'd seen bigger swells in a bath.

So where's the dog now? I said.

You didn't see it back there by the roadside anywhere? he asked. Must've wandered off to chew on someone else.

Oh so it bit you too.

Not hard he said nonchalantly. Not enough to break the skin.

While he stood there talking his hair was starting to dry in the sun it poked up in a little quiff like Tin Tin's and the more he spoke the more it seemed to stick up. Kid's fringe was Pinocchio's nose.

Fine don't tell me what really happened I said. In the distance a boat engine rumbled.

You're in my year at school he said.

You're in mine I corrected.

You shouldn't call yourself Red not with hair like that he said.

(Like people might not notice the colour if I had a different name.)

Yeah well you shouldn't go swimming without floaties there Duncan Armstrong but we don't always know what's good for us I said.

Stevie Madigan grinned.

He was a weird kid. He was wearing his school shorts and his knees stuck out from paddle-pop-stick legs his ribs were raised like railway sleepers. And yet you could tell Stevie Madigan came from a good home and that his mum must've loved him half to death you could see it in his school shirt which was lying on the jetty and which somehow still had crisp folds in it that thing had been ironed so many times I'd seen less permanent tattoos than those pleats his shoes were polished to military standard and standing there in the early-morning sunshine half drowned and flecked with bits of his own vomit Stevie Madigan still managed to look like he'd been scrubbed with an entire canful of Mr Sheen.

I knew Mrs Madigan everyone did she ran the bookshop on Mann Street in town not a surf shop or a cake shop not even a newsagency you didn't get that many bookshops on the coast.

Your mum sells books I said.

Your dad thinks he's John Wayne.

What no he doesn't what are you talking about my dad doesn't think he's John Wayne.

Nothing wrong with that Stevie said. My grandpa used to think he was Captain Esteban Pasquale you know from *Zorro* Mum made him a cape and everything it was black on the outside and red underneath she even stitched bobbles round the edges.

I'm happy for your grandpa but my dad doesn't think he's John Wayne.

Then how come he was sitting on the steps outside the TAB after closing on Tuesday singing how he was.

Was what.

John Wayne.

Jesus Christ I said.

Nah definitely John Wayne he said helpfully.

That's just a song it doesn't mean anything I said hotly (when really what it meant was that Race 22 hadn't come in and Sid had blown his last cent until payday and he'd come home in a filthy mood and kicked a hole in the laundry wall but Stevie Madigan didn't need to know all that).

Sure Stevie said.

He rubbed the back of his skinny neck thoughtfully and then he said: Anyway it'd be worse if your dad *did* think he was Jesus – you don't even get a bobble cape with that.

—

I never expected any reward for fishing Stevie out of the bay it never occurred to me to ask for one although Sid wasn't averse to the idea was pretty partial to it in fact never look a gift horse in any orifice Sid liked to say.

But when Mrs Madigan showed up on our doorstep two days later and presented me with a book from her bookshop on Mann Street I wasn't disappointed *a book* and not just any book but a book like I'd never seen before its cover was the most beguiling dark-green hardback but soft to touch and the smell was intoxicating the smell of damp wool of library stacks I could of held it to my nostrils for a week. The cover was embossed with gilt lettering that curled each toe in ecstasy it was the most incredible thing that I'd ever seen honest to God the best thing I'd ever held.

She looks like you like a mini Medusa said Mrs Madigan as I turned a page.

That watercolour picture was of a fierce-eyed woman she had a tangled mess of snakes writhing round her head instead of hair. But then Mrs Madigan had three boys at home so I was guessing her whole house was a tangled mess of things and that she didn't mean anything by it and anyway I could tell it was intended as a compliment because of the way she fingered one of my red curls unfurled it and admired its colour in the sunshine.

Thanks Mrs Madigan I said.

Call me Lorraine she replied.

And that curl rebelled from her fingers then bounced back into its messy nest.

A book? Sid tried to drum up some enthusiasm. A book's better than a hole in the head you want to hang onto that Ruby Tuesday you never know could be worth something one day.

But there was no way I was selling *The Golden Treasury of Greek Mythology*.

No Sid admitted later when it was just me and him. No market for that around here.

—

Just about the only lottery Sid couldn't hack was the National Service Lottery yeah compulsory military service i.e. *conscription*. Three hundred and sixty-six wooden marbles each one numbered and checked and chucked in a Tattersall's barrel every ball was some mug's birthday. And if your number came up then you'd blow out the candles and unwrap your uniform happy birthday you're off to Vietnam that's right if your number came up you got two years' compulsory military service happy birthday the death lottery they called it.

Those lotteries were held twice a year from 1965 to 1972 and if you were twenty and male then your number was in the barrel they were drawn in the boardroom of the Department of Labour and National Service in Melbourne where those little wooden marbles barely bigger than your thumb were pulled out by some big d█ck.

Sid's birthday was drawn out on the first of March 1966 yeah lucky old fourteenth of June. Sid's number was up or so it seemed for a while there hard to imagine my old man with a gun no you've never seen anyone less likely to join the army never seen anyone less suited to the job. Sid'd use his bayonet to lift baby birds back to their nests yeah he'd be rescuing flipped beetles in the trenches either that or he'd be running betting rings like his life depended on it wanna put money on whether D Company will be the first to return from patrol wanna have a flutter on the first bloke sent home in a body bag.

Only Sid never had to try his luck at Long Tan no he never saw service in Nui Dat instead he saw a doctor who said Sid's gout meant he couldn't serve on account of the danger it posed to Sid's kidneys. What. Would he be drinking with the Viet Cong.

Still that's how Sid avoided the Vietnam War by having gout in his left big toe and when the doctor thanked Sid for the envelope full of cash he said it wasn't necessary but he put it in his pocket all the same.

Sergeant Healy found himself a good doctor too no surprise that his doctor was a friend of the family and that friend of the family deemed Sergeant Healy unfit for duty. (Back then Sergeant Healy hadn't qualified as a constable yet but that didn't matter it didn't matter if he was Krusty the Clown no one got out of conscription on account of their job not unless they were a minister you know like a priest and let me tell you something for nothing Sergeant Healy was no man of the cloth.) Instead it took a phone call from his dad to get the sarge off the hook and even then I bet he resented the inconvenience yeah even though he didn't have to hustle like Sid did I'm sure it killed the sergeant that he and Sid got the exact same treatment in the end oh the injustice of that would of stung.

—

Funny enough the thing that makes me ache for Sid's ugly mug is when I hear someone talk about their plans for the future who'd of guessed I might miss Sid's mad schemes.

Sid had plenty of ideas alright like the time he was going to hire a metal detector and spend the tourist season fossicking along the beachfronts for dropped coins or lost wedding rings or temporarily misplaced ingots of gold or whatever else he really believed was out there. Or the time he was going to undercut the ferry operator and carry tourists to Woy Woy in his two-man tinny for a quarter of the price of a ferry ticket plus Sid's gondola singing thrown in free. Or the time he was going to get rich buying up all those priceless collectors' items he imagined were handed in at the pawn shop in East Gosford each week or like that time he was going to make his fortune manufacturing industrial levels of home brew that even the White Hart refused to serve to customers or the time he thought the future was Betamax or the time he bought a share in a racehorse that turned out to be legally blind or the time he was going to run a white goods delivery service without a truck or a trolley and no goods.

Up here for thinking and down there for dancing Sid used to say and he'd tap his head and do a passable soft-shoe shuffle but then dancing wasn't Sid's downfall and neither was dreaming no Sid wasn't lacking in the ideas department.

Execution was what let Sid down.

Sid's best business venture was the one that was just around the corner glittering elusive unreal *that* was the one that would make us a motza yeah the one that was coming up next. And it wasn't just that Sid didn't like hard work – though there was that – it was more like work with all its boring ordinariness its routines its drudgery its everyday smallnesses was somehow an insult to Sid's big dreams and big dreams were everything to Sid.

The best times were when I'd lie in the backyard and look up at the clouds and listen to Sid's harebrained schemes yeah those were the best times. Not that our backyard was anything to boast about there were empty petrol cans in a pile by the carport and a metal bed frame half buried by the fence and fish scales like snowflakes below the concrete feeding trough and a fridge carcass open-mouthed in the chickweeds. But the bluegrass was long and the shade was deep and sometimes pelicans would careen overhead pale-pink-and-white specks so far above the earth their span was as small as your fingernail if you held your thumb up to the sky.

Sid would sit himself there in the driver's seat of whatever car was in the carport that week with the door flung open and the seat reclined so it was just about horizontal like he was poolside in the Bahamas and not lounging in the carport where the jack-pipe pylons were rusted into place and the corrugated PVC roof had long gone opaque so that looking up was like peering at the world through cloudy cataracted eyes.

And he'd lie there with his hands propped behind his head his feet propped up on the steering wheel his big toe fiddling mindlessly with the knobs and dials on the dash his mouth never pausing either.

Carp Sid would say. Now you're talking.

He spoke like he was continuing some previous conversation like you'd already signed up to his dream. His face was leathery from too much time in the sun his chin was beardy but his head was bowling-ball smooth.

Plenty of people that'd pay good money for carp Ruby Tuesday.

What people?

Restaurant people tourist people. They're a big fish carp – game fishermen could use them as bait.

Are you serious?

But that's not the best bit.

Tell me what's the best bit?

What would you say if I told you you'd get paid *twice* for selling carp once by the customer and once by the government for eradicating an introduced species!

I'd say you're full of carp.

Ah Rubes and he'd look away rubbing his head ruefully and you knew he was trying not to laugh.

Carp are pests they're the rabbits of the river system I'm performing a community service Sid'd say then.

And nothing in it for yourself?

Well maybe a little he'd concede his toes dancing across the dash his mouth splitting into a grin.

You'll see Rube one day you'll see.

Despite it you couldn't stop yourself from smiling he really did think it could happen.

—

Sid's neighbours growing up were teetotallers which is a joke when you think how much of an effect that had on young Sid yeah what an impression that left. The Christies didn't drink but Mr Christie was the manager of the sawmill at Wyong and each Christmas that mill owner gave Mr Christie a bottle of Teacher's Highland Cream and Mrs Christie would take that bottle and put it reverentially at the back of the laundry cupboard until every so often when she'd pull it down and get a rag and use it to clean the windows that's right Mrs Christie used scotch whisky to polish her picture windows said it gave them a lovely shine. Only before Mrs Christie's windows could dry (probably before Mrs Christie got that bottle safely back in the laundry cupboard) Sid McCoy from next door would appear from nowhere and give those windows a second going-over with his tongue. Bit of reverse spit and polish. Sid reckons that's how he got a taste for the good stuff from licking those Christie windows clean. Sid could imbibe half a bottle before Mrs Christie noticed more if she did the window insides as well.

—

The house Sid grew up in got knocked down to make way for holiday rentals. Back when Sid was a kid that place was a single-level fibro joint just like every other house on the street but now it's a block of flats and investment bankers and insurance wankers and God knows which other rich pricks come up from Sydney each January to stay in the units to enjoy a swim in the kidney-shaped pool. They sling their beach towels over the balcony railings when they're in residence like raising the flag at f■king Buckingham Palace.

It was the boon docks back in Sid's day no TV I don't know probably no electricity not even a sewer connection no wonder Sid thought he was king of the world when Pook lifted a VCR for us that one time.

And they did lift stuff it's true Pook and Sparra and Chook and Sid they occasionally helped themselves but then it's not like anyone else was queuing up to give them a hand not like the government or the welfare people no none of them were offering a leg up. And nicking things like VCRs and dumped white goods the occasional used car was hardly hurting anyone not when compared to what Sergeant Healy and his mates took from us yeah Sticky Fingers Healy stealing our happiness our dignity taking away my family yeah flexing his pig muscles for kicks.

—

Like the time the cops showed up at our place it was early evening the last rays of sun slanting through the trees the bay was bright henna red. It was the summer of the Datsun it was the summer Sid first drove his car home from the dealership in Wyoming singing 'Hi-Yo Silver' all the way.

But when the cops pulled up at our place that evening they didn't come with any noise no siren wailing they didn't even arrive with the sound of their two-way radio drifting out their open windows no they sidled up quietly slunk in like maybe the pair of them had something to hide like maybe they weren't there at all.

They drove right up to where I was squatting in front of the carport came so close their front bumper almost touched me I didn't flinch I knew that they'd seen me squatting in the dirt yeah I'd met their eyes through the windscreen.

Across the road at number six Mr Anders looked up from where he was watering his dahlias and decided it was time to call it a day. Mr Anders knew he hadn't broken any water restrictions that he was entitled to water his dahlias any time after six using a handheld hose what's more he knew the cops couldn't care less about water restrictions yeah they were strictly the domain of the council even so when Mr Anders saw that cop car pull up at our place he decided his dahlias had had a decent drink he turned off his tap and left his hose where it was snaking across the grass and he disappeared inside.

Two of them climbed out of the cop car that day pale-blue shirts chequer-band caps their gun holsters shiny reptilian. A big cop and an even bigger one is how I remember them and the bigger one smoking a cigarette.

Your daddy home?

I'd been poking around in the dirt looking for more sandstone shards to use as chalk when they drove up and before that I'd been happy drawing on the floor of the carport but now I wiped my hands guiltily on my haunches.

Whaddya wanna know for? I remember saying.

Because Sid always said just because trouble comes visiting doesn't mean you have to offer it a place to sit down.

Well now that's big talk from a little lady the cop said only he paused too long before he landed on the word 'lady' and the bigger cop sniggered to himself.

I said is your daddy home he repeated.

Beside him his mate blew cigarette smoke sideways.

See for yourself whydontcha I said and I stayed down in the dust while they towered above me the two of them like a dirty big eclipse blocking the last of the sun their patrol car blocked our driveway too. They'd parked so close I could feel heat radiating off the front bumper I wasn't going to be the one to move.

The big one crouched down and looked me dead in the eye. Tang of stale smoke and spicy meat.

I've got a better idea why don't you go get him for me.

He spoke carefully. Then he turned to his mate who flicked his cigarette butt so it landed right beside my bare toes we all watched it burning in the dirt.

Siiid! I hollered because I was rattled now. Siiiid!

The crouching cop smirked.

I could hear canned laughter coming from the TV inside it was *Wheel of Fortune* time and Sid always watched *Wheel of Fortune* while he read the form guide. *Spin the wheel buy a vowel pick a winner.*

Siiiid! I shouted again but I still didn't move. Instead the cop stood up and when he did he lost his balance for a split second he wobbled then he steadied himself on the front bumper but it was enough and I saw it and what's more he saw I saw it. I covered a puff of laugh with my hand.

Ruby? Sid shouted and the flyscreen door flew open canned laughter followed him onto the porch. Ruby?

He clocked the cops and froze.

What's this? he said.

His shorts refused to be seen alongside his skinny hips and he hoicked them up as he walked his t-shirt flapped behind him those blue thongs slapped as he strode.

Sidney McCoy!

The first cop raised his arms like he was welcoming an old friend and then he took a step towards the porch and as he did he brought his boot down on the hand I'd just used to hide my laugh he did it with such agonising care rolling from heel to black toecap and holding it there before lifting it up like it never happened there's no way it was accidental.

What do you blokes want? Sid said suspiciously.

He hadn't seen that cop tread on my fingers.

In the dirt I turned away and cradled my hand to my chest oh I squeezed it rubbed it against the thin cotton of my t-shirt I wrapped it up in my terry-towelling shorts anything to stop myself from running crying to Sid and to have him pick me up tug my earlobe make a joke make it better but nobody was looking at me anyway the two cops had their eyes trained on Sid and Sid was eyeing them right back as they walked over to their patrol car and leaned against the bonnet their arms folded across their pale-blue stomachs their legs crossed ridiculously at their ankles. The bigger one broke his stare to glance down at his mate he was waiting for instructions it seemed.

The bonnet of their patrol car read WY for Wyoming Local Area Command I might of only been learning my letters back in those days but I could reel off all the vehicle bonnet codes of the local area cop cars GF Gosford YT Yattalunga BW

Brisbane Water yeah I didn't need to sing the alphabet song to know what W and Y meant WY spelt trouble it spelt pull your head in if you know what's good for you.

They'd come out of their way to get to our house on Jabiru Avenue it was a good twenty-minute drive for Sergeant Healy's men to get from Wyoming to here and what's more they had to drive past police stations at Gosford and Yattalunga along the way. No not what you'd call their own jurisdiction hardly sh▮tting in their own backyard.

That big cop said nice evening for it or something similar and Sid replied nice evening for what.

You're all business Sidney I remember that cop complaining. What got no time to make conversation?

Not with you blokes Sid said darkly.

And the big cop said you want to watch that mouth of yours doesn't land you in hot water. That's unless it already has.

And in the dirt I crossed my fingers one on top of the other pinkie over ring finger and tall man over index. I crossed them on my good hand and then I crossed them painfully on my injured hand and when I'd done crossing them I wished that they'd leave my dad alone that they wouldn't lay a single hand on him.

Then Sid said choof off Ruby get inside the house but I refused.

Go on skedaddle he said.

And I refused again and he said flipping get inside plus he called me Red as well.

So I stood up and I held my sore hand gingerly by my side I wasn't going to give them the satisfaction of knowing I was hurt. I stalked past Sid and flung the flyscreen door so hard it banged against the wall but before I went in I turned and I raised my sore hand to those cops and with effort I gave them the finger.

Whoooeeee she's a fiery one.

Nice manners you're teaching your kid there McCoy.

She got a mouth to match? Bet she has bet it's hot as a Fisherman's Friend.

And honestly what sort of paedo says that about a kid. The pair of them carried on like pork chops while Sid stood stony on the front lawn and across the road Mr Anders's dahlias dripped delicately after their drink down the street a dog barked half-heartedly.

—

I went and sat cross-legged on the lounge-room floor and peered out at the front yard through a gap in the terylene curtains and from there I saw Sid run a hand over his bald head the way he did when he was thinking or plotting or some days both he worked up a lovely shine scheming some new idea or other yeah usually it was a good sign if Sid's noggin gleamed (or a bad one depending on your perspective). Now though he rubbed his head warily as if he was trying to remember something like he was trying to put his finger on something other than his own lustrous skull.

He seemed to say: I might of.

And: So what of it if I did?

Then the bigger cop said something I couldn't hear.

No crime in talking Sid said and he was getting animated. Strike a light what *your* blokes did to my car was the crime and not me speaking about it.

Because everyone knew Sid had been down the pub complaining how the cops keyed his car.

There was more talk then but I couldn't hear it and more rubbing of Sid's sheeny head and then one cop straightened up from where he'd been leaning on the bonnet of the patrol car and wandered over to Sid's Datsun it was parked in the concrete carport.

That Datsun shone. Sid had polished it to within an inch of its life took a rag to it every week gotta look after your things Ruby Tuesday he'd tell me. He used WD-40 in its happy blue-and-yellow can Sid loved WD-40 would've put the stuff on his cereal and drunk it in his tea if he could of. Yeah he sprayed it on the windscreen to stop insects from sticking and on the duco to clean bird poo off he used it to lube the spark plugs and keep moisture off the alternators and distributors and shift stuck nuts and God knows what else he polished with the stuff a kid didn't like to ask yeah just about the only thing Sid couldn't do with his WD-40 was fix that scratch from the cops but not because he didn't try. That scar stretched almost the whole length of the Datsun from fender to arsehole and Sid couldn't make it disappear.

Now that cop bent down and ran a finger along the scratch he followed it from the driver's door all the way to the petrol tank flap at the back. He was the cop that had stood on my fingers but beneath his feet now was the rainbow I'd been drawing on the concrete it was monochrome I only had white to work with it arced away from the rear tyre like speed lines in a cartoon.

He stood then and said something I couldn't hear what but it was the sort of something that made Sid throw his arms in the air and mutter to himself disgust scrawled across his long face. Then it was the bigger cop's turn to push off the bonnet of the patrol car he straightened up and walked around the back of the car he popped the boot and took something out and when he reappeared it was with a sledgehammer.

Sid's leather face paled.

Now the finger-treading cop moved away from the Datsun as the second cop approached the car he held the sledgehammer by its wooden handle and the two of them were like little balsawood figures that moved in the clock in our dining room the tall man and his tiny wooden wife dancing in a circle whenever it hit o'clock only there was no chiming now no striking the hour it was Sid's Datsun that got walloped.

That cop swung the sledgehammer over his shoulder and brought it down like a pendulum straight into the driver's side door that Datsun crumpled and Sid did too he slumped to his knees his face falling his hands dropping uselessly to his sides and inside the house I shouted then I clapped my hands over my mouth but I shouldn't have worried no one was listening to me.

Again and again and again that big pig brought the sledgehammer down on the Datsun he swung it with all its ugly force its wooden handle windrushing its heavy head butting into the metal and Sid's driver's side door all dented then punctured yeah it was ripped open like a can of creamed corn. And when he'd finished with that door he moved along to the next one working methodically he swung and crunched swung and crunched next the rear passenger door then the lid of the boot then the other rear door and then on to the front passenger door and when he got to the bonnet the noise was shocking those dull whumps those shrieks of metal but worse than that was the wordless misery leaking from inside Sid.

When there were no panels left to destroy and one passenger window had shattered and so had the windscreen and one side mirror dangled loose the tall cop stepped back and lowered his sledgehammer he stood breathing hard beside Sid's car and the fist of his hammer rested on my chalk rainbow I mean on the Datsun's speed lines yeah it was pinning the car down yeah holding it back that Datsun wasn't fleeing the scene.

Then the smaller cop wiped his hands on his navy trousers as though he'd been the one doing all the work as if he'd ever swung a hammer. Then he turned and said something to Sid I couldn't hear it from inside but whatever it was it must've been bloody funny because that cop just about burst a blood vessel laughing at his own joke yeah he was at risk of having a coronary.

And the whole time he was laughing I felt like I might be sick because it was my fault that tall cop smashed Sid's car all that buckled metal all that shattered glass yeah my fault they bashed Sid's car instead of Sid because I was the one who wished it and I only did it because I didn't want them to hurt Sid but look there see they'd destroyed him anyway they didn't need to lay a finger on him to do that no I'd never seen Sid look so crushed.

—

That Datsun was done for. Dun-coloured done for there was no way to drive Sid's gold car now. No more 'Hi-Yo Silver' down the freeway for that Datsun no more hi-yo golden away. And later when Sid found his tongue again yeah long after the cops had driven off and Sid had come inside and the two of us had sat on the brown lounge and watched the end of *Wheel of Fortune* though the form guide had slid quietly to the floor yeah that's when Sid told me how the cops claimed his Datsun was unroadworthy because of that scratch down the side.

What's that?

What's what?

Unroadworthy what is it.

Means a car isn't good enough to drive Sid explained. They reckoned that because the Datsun had been keyed that it wasn't fit to drive.

But when Sid said there was nothing unroadworthy about the Datsun and it was the cops that scratched it anyway so why didn't they shove their road rules up their ■■■ well that's when the tall cop got the sledgehammer out.

See? They said to Sid when they left. Told you it was unroadworthy.

—

Sid said they were mongrels oh they were low as snakes' ar■es and Sergeant Healy was the worst of the lot that Sergeant Healy couldn't blow the froth off a schooner Sid reckoned he couldn't find a f■■■ in a brothel and that's why Sergeant Healy sent those two thugs to our place yeah to do his dirty work for him. So you see Sid is of this place and he's *because* of this place you can't ever separate the two. Sid did the things he did because of the things that were done to him and if you're going to try to blame Sid well then you can all shoulder some of that particular liability because you're the ones that made Sid turn out that way yeah you can all carry that can.

—

Like I said after the Datsun came the Sandman which Sid was just minding for Chook and later there was the Torana although that vanished after Sid saw a man about a dog yeah we only had that car for three weeks. But even when we didn't have a car Sid and I muddled along alright yeah we got a lift with his mates or we rode our bikes or we simply stayed home it wasn't hard nothing was too hard for Sid and me in those days so long as the cops gave us a wide berth.

Sometimes they'd go for months without showing their ugly pig faces and during those times Sid and me we'd do alright I never wanted for anything walking from room to room in that once-white weatherboard on Jabiru Avenue you could stumble across a chicken coop in the lounge room or go through the saloon doors and into the kitchen and there's a box of *Making Michael Jackson's Thriller* VHS tapes cellophane wrappers still intact or eight cartons of surfboard wax at 200 tubs of wax per carton teetering next to the toilet. Once we had an actual kitchen sink on the dining table for months. Another time the bathtub stored industrial amounts of pool chlorine packed and stacked in fluoro-blue buckets. Yeah there were car parts and plywood planks and nine rolls of lino and a box of broken windscreen wipers and a crate of Queensland numberplates and a microwave oven in every room each one unboxed and bearing the name Toshiba but left unplugged and unspinning on the floor.

And if you asked Sid where something came from then he'd smile enigmatically and say where does anyone come from Rube.

And if you asked him where it was going to then he'd say same place we're all headed sunshine: to the big rodeo in the sky.

And if you cracked it and said no seriously what other kid has to step over a lawnmower carburettor to turn on the flipping TV? *What's it actually for?* Well then Sid'd give you a long and gasbagging explanation of how a carburettor regulates the air-to-fuel ratio of internal combustion engines and he'd carry on winding you up until you'd just about combust yourself.

—

The design of the house was a loop an overcrowded fire hazard of a loop like a mouth crammed with too many teeth. The front door opened into a corridor which led to the lounge room which led to the dining room which led to the kitchen and then back into the corridor through a pair of swinging saloon doors they started at hip height and petered out just above my head their wooden slats louvred like letterbox slots. Don't let the doors hit you on the way out Sid would say when I stormed out of the kitchen in a huff it's hard to say whether those doors begot Sid's cowboy craze or was it the other way round does the chicken come before the egg does the cowboy make the saloon.

Yeah number nine Jabiru Avenue was one chock-a-block circle one long vicious cycle of boxed-up junk just fallen off the back of a truck plus two bedrooms and a bathroom tacked onto one side. Sid used to walk that loop like he was trotting laps at Saratoga Racecourse his long lanky legs his faithful blue rubber thongs he'd walk circuits of the house talking and pontificating and picking at boxes till he wore a path in the shagpile.

Sometimes he walked the loop playing his violin his bow arm pumping his body swaying his left hand fingering deftly. He'd walk and he'd play because playing on its own wasn't enough movement for Sid and it wasn't just the fact that he couldn't stand still that made Sid an unlikely-looking violinist. There was the bushranger beard and the short Stubbies shorts and the 1976 Mount Panorama t-shirt that was holey under one arm or maybe it was the nicotine-stained digits that danced up and down the black fingerboard yeah Sid looked ripe to play the pokies or play darts anything other than jump in an orchestra pit but jeez he knew his way around a violin.

Any cowboy can carry a tune he'd say. Trouble comes when he tries to unload it.

But Sid could unload a tune he could unpack gigues and gavottes and sonatas and allegros he could deadset discharge a concerto at twenty paces. Pep taught him how to play must've been one of the things Pep picked up at his school in the city and what Pep learned he passed on to Sid along with an expensive Mendini violin which somehow Sid hadn't hocked yet yeah you'd never know it from the exterior but us McCoys we had real class.

Even if Sid did sometimes have a ciggie while he played.

We had class and also we had everything a kid could want: food on the table cold Cottee's in the fridge. From the minute I woke up and Sid presented me with tea and toast two pieces of the finest white sliced that the supermarket could muster there was always plenty to eat more tomato sauce sandwiches than a kid could wish for and more rissoles 'n' tomato sauce and pie 'n' sauce and sauce 'n' sauce with sauce on the side and then every year when my birthday rolled around a frozen Sara Lee Chocolate Bavarian Cake from the factory out at Lisarow would materialise in the freezer at least Sid didn't put sauce on that.

The other thing that would show up at birthday time and Christmas time and the Queen's Birthday long weekend and just about every other time of the year like they didn't have a home to go to was the Yattalunga Cricket Club B Division 'Rovers'. There was Boof and Ferret and Macca and Jezza and Kezza and Sparra and Pook. Kev too sometimes. And always Chook yeah he was practically rusted on. Our front flyscreen was like a revolving door for blokes of a certain age seeking refuge from their lives it was as if they liked the fact there were no females living here except for me like I counted anyway. They'd turn up with a slab and expect nothing in return just some company and so Sid would settle down on the back patio with whichever B Division stray had wandered in that day and they'd drink and smoke and set the world to rights I loved to listen to them talk.

She's got more front than Woolworths.

He's a showbag full of crap.

He's all sausage and no sizzle.

He's all tip and no iceberg.

She's as game as Ned Kelly.

He's as rough as hessian undies.

He's as popular as a snake in a lucky dip.

She's as lucky as a ticket in the meat raffle.

They're potholes the pair of them always in the road.

I wouldn't piss on him if he was on fire.

I wouldn't go to his funeral if I was the undertaker.

Yeah Sid and his mates might have had sh█-all to say but they always put it so eloquently.

And Stevie and I would sit on the back steps looking out over the yard with its empty petrol cans and its concrete trough for gutting fish and its Frigidaire fridge corroding in the weeds and we'd drink the dregs from the Rovers' discarded empties and we'd imitate the way that they talked.

You've got a face like a sucked mango.

You've got a face like a chewed Mintie.

You've got a face like a smashed crab.

You've got a face like a battered sav.

You're as ugly as a kicked-in biscuit tin.

You're as ugly as a hat full of a█eholes.

You're a freckle fart from Kmart.

Then Stevie would clutch his chest and slump against the handrail that was barely holding itself up let alone Stevie too and he'd say that cuts Red that really hurts me here and he'd stab a finger at his puny chest and I'd say get your hand off it Stevie and by 'it' you know I never meant Stevie's heart.

The other thing the B Division Rovers did apart from

hanging around at our place farting and drinking and leaving their empties lying around for Stevie and me to finish off was the annual Kangol Cup. The Kangol Cup what a testament to male ingenuity and endurance yeah what a celebration of macho bull■. Sure it might've looked like any other one-day cricket match between the Yattalunga B Division Rovers and the neighbouring Kincumber C Division starting with the first over at nine am and first beers at quarter past but it was so much more than that. The Kangol Cup was about triumph and pride about mateship and skill but most of all it was about burning an old pair of Chook's Kangol underpants to make their own homegrown version of international test cricket's Ashes yeah to make actual charred undies to put in a tin mug for the winning side to take home.

Except that nobody from either side ever went home on the day of the Kangol Cup they played twenty overs or until the Esky ran dry whichever came first and then they retired to Davistown RSL to continue drinking and then when they were kicked out of there at closing they rolled around to our place or Chook's place or wherever there were beers in the fridge once after the Kangol Cup I didn't see Sid for two days.

But during that early part of the morning of the Cup yeah those first few golden hours yeah that Datsun-coloured time with the light dribbling in through the trees and the magpies cardle-wardelling at the starlings on the telegraph wires and the methodical *thwack thwack thwack* of leather against imitation willow and the swears of dismay when silly mid-off drops a sitter yeah early Saturday morning what a time to be alive yeah before the Rovers got shickered.

And those Rovers would wave and chiack in the field for my benefit they were Red's Rovers during that first innings yeah they were all mine and I was their mascot their good-luck charm their teeny queen perched on the transformer box by the edge of the oval sitting on my green throne my hair uncombed and billowing in the breeze my legs crossed happily beneath me. Until the point when the pile of empties outstripped the run rate three times over and then I'd take myself off home.

Some years Stevie would come with me and the two of us would sit together on the utility box or we'd sit side by side on two blue Eskies our cans of Fanta balanced on the grass between us. We must've looked like passengers sitting across the bus aisle from one another yeah pensioners on the ten-oh-six to Terrigal.

—

Honestly though Stevie and I weren't on the same bus so to speak we never were if you want to know the truth. Yeah even though we were in the same year at school same suburb and everything Stevie went to school every day with a *Star Wars* lunchbox and matching thermos while I took my sandwich loose in a supermarket bag also his attendance record almost doubled mine also he wore a school shirt from Lowes with the actual school crest embroidered on the top pocket while I wore whatever generic green-and-yellow clothes Sid siphoned from Best & Less but despite all that I still ran rings round Stevie academically just don't ask Stevie he'd say it was a closer-run thing.

—

Never let the truth get in the way of a good story that was Stevie's motto.

—

Stevie said: You know how West Gosford McDonald's has that kids' party room decked out like a Ye Olde train carriage you know the one Rube? Do you know how the carriage came to be sitting in that paddock behind the Drive-Thru?

Stevie said: It happened after a passenger train derailed there one night did you know that I bet you didn't.

Stevie said: Yeah the train line used to go right through that paddock there I've seen the old sleepers and everything.

Stevie said: You know once I climbed from Terrigal to the Haven via the rocks. I did it with my brothers you weren't there you wouldn't remember.

Stevie said: You know once I saw a kid put detergent in the fountain at Fountain Plaza and the cops came and took him away. The newspapers never reported it no they never said a word I don't think they ever saw that kid again.

You know once I saw a stingray attack a shark you know once I got an Allan Langer footy card but I didn't care I swapped it for Paul Harragon you know once one of my brothers broke into the Reptile Park and freed all the lizards you know my uncle wrote the lyrics to 'Eye of the Tiger' you know I'm related to Michael J. Fox you know in the holidays my mum's taking us to Australia's Wonderland and I'm gunna ride on the Bush Beast you know a skink can regrow its own head.

Sure thing Stevie Wonder whatever you reckon. Whatever you say Stevie Wonder.

—

Mrs Madigan would've had no idea what she started when she gave that book to me how could she but she sure set wheels in motion when she showed up on the doorstep and handed me *The Golden Treasury of Greek Mythology* in all its green-cover rich-gilt glory.

It's not that I wasn't a reader beforehand I was I read compulsively *Harp in the South Pippi Longstocking True Grit The Grapes of Wrath The Well The Catcher in the Rye Came Back to Show You I Could Fly The Children's Bach* I pored over Sid's fishing catalogues too I didn't care what I read so long as it had words (even if some of those fishing words were: bunghole and flange and bait raped).

But nothing else I read could touch *The Golden Treasury of Greek Mythology* no nothing else even came close I loved that book God I read it like a bible I can still feel the weight of it in my hands.

The pages of *The Golden Treasury of Greek Mythology* were a hypnotic jumble a mess of myths and stories and all in syllables my tongue hadn't met yet and if there was any sequence to the gods and the goddesses and the semi-divine and the spirits and the giants and the creatures all crammed inside well then I couldn't find the logic. It was like they'd stumbled down

Olympus and just joined the back of the queue yeah like some sort of Delphic Centrelink. There was Zeus and Apollo and Dionysus and Hades there was Hermes and Eros and Nyx I read about Erebus and Thanatos and Agon and Alala (I discovered Nike was the goddess of victory and not just basketball shoes). But the ones that got me yeah the ones that stopped me dead in my tracks were the Keres. *Keres Keres Keres* I used to say it like I was saying Kerry's or even Kelly's the word morphed and grew in my head. I said it so much it became an incantation.

Even the word itself sounded like *curse*.

The Keres were female death spirits the Greek goddesses of violent deaths. Beautiful malevolent vicious the Keres were black fates they were winged agents of fury and violence materialising on the battlefield at the moment of Death yeah hovering over Death's shoulder waiting like vultures like vampires ready to scoop up the bodies they were bloodthirsty women of battle.

But the Keres didn't kill according to *The Golden Treasury of Greek Mythology* no they only showed up when Death was inevitable when it was the only card left in the pack and then they feasted on the bloody remains those Keres knew a thing or two about destiny.

—

And in the watercolour picture in my book the Keres were glamorous demigods all barrel curls and eyes sloeblack and wings crowblack. And I guess it was the curls that caused the association the curls or maybe the sound of their name but it got to the point where I couldn't think about those Keres without picturing the poster of Grace Kelly in the hairdresser's window in town. That poster had been souvenired from a *Women's Weekly* magazine commemoration special several eons ago and it showed Grace Kelly in a satin evening gown it was from her *To Catch a Thief* years. There she was with her eyes smouldering her curls shiny in the car headlights as punters pulled in to go to the TAB next door. Or I'd think of Kerri-Anne Kennerley from *Good Morning Australia* who Sid woke up to every day with her big bouncy TV hair and her big TV smile and those legs Sid said they were the best pins in the business. And sometimes I'd think about my dead mum too she wasn't a Kelly or a Kerri like the others but she was beautiful enough to be yeah every photo I've got of Mum she's teeth smiling curls coiling. *Mum.*

And between Mum and Grace Kelly and Kerri-Anne Kennerley between those three and the Keres in my book all those bouncing barrel curls got tangled up in my head until I had a small army of beautiful avengers up there flying around in my imagination yeah I swear they got wedged in my head.

NEXT

When I was still at high school Sid's mate Jim 'Chook' Fowler got Sid a job at the power station. And even though it meant Sid missed seeing Kerri-Anne Kennerley on the box each morning because now he left the house while Kerri-Anne was probably still in makeup probably still puffing her perm and even though Sid and Chook had to drive an hour up the Pacific Highway through Gosford and Wyoming and Niagara Park and Kangy Angy and all the way to San Remo and then take a left off Scenic Drive because you need to detour a long way from the scenic side of life before you arrive there at Munmorah Power Station yeah despite that Sid figured a job was a step up from the dole because even Sid wasn't that stupid.

This was the 1990s remember and they'd closed Gosford abattoir that one Easter it was the biggest employer in the area until they shut up shop on Maundy Thursday leaving a thousand blokes standing outside the gates with nothing but a sack of valedictory lamb shanks one sack per person plus the prospect of going home for the long weekend to tell their wives they no longer had a job and their dogs they no longer had a bone supply and their mothers-in-law they'd be eating lamb instead of fish on that particular Good Friday but what was so f█████ good about it anyway.

Before that it was the shipyards and before that the brick company.

Yeah they'd closed after almost half a century of business here and now the region had an unemployment rate that was through the roof and a living standard that was falling through the floor so you know what our government did oh they started building shopping centres as if we had money to spend at the shops seriously what kind of sick joke is that. They built Kincumber Shopping Centre though that was partly paid for by the tennis star John 'Newk' Newcombe remember him then they built Deepwater Plaza over at Woy Woy with its Fosseys and its Super Kmart which later became an ordinary Kmart yeah not so super after all. Deepwater Plaza was opened at an official ceremony by Spike Milligan's mum yeah Flo and then three years later they built Central Coast Fair at Erina the biggest single-level f██k-off shopping centre in the southern hemisphere with its drive-in and its Grace Bros. and all of the rest of it I have to admit we hung out there a lot but just in the food court you know. Meanwhile in Mann Street where the Madigans have their bookshop the strip's just about abandoned empty shops empty buildings derelict offices BYO tumbleweed.

Even Sid's job at the power station was just to wind things up so the station could close down.

Munmorah used to be the biggest coal-fired power station in New South Wales it had four turbo generators and it was linked by conveyor belt to Chain Valley Bay Colliery and Endeavour Colliery and Munmorah State Coal Mine and Wallarah Colliery and Wyee State Colliery it supplied nearly half the state's power for all those years but now even Munmorah was calling it a day yeah production was being wound right back two units were being relegated to emergency use only so Sid and Chook and the rest of them were brought in to get things ready for closure *remediation* was what the foreman called it *cleaning up other people's sh▮t* were the words Sid used.

Sid didn't relish the idea of paid employment no offence to Chook who got him the job but Sid hated the eight o'clock starts and he hated all the hours that followed. He hated knowing he was missing Kerri-Anne. Still Sid went off each day in Chook's rusty Sandman his beard washed his face shiny as a cheap suit his hard hat sitting submissive on his knees. Yeah the two of them went off and worked in the shadow of those two towering chimneystacks each one emblazoned with the name Vectra Electrical like two huge fingers raised by management at their workers yeah up yours to those men working down in the yard. It was there that Sid and Chook and everyone else spent the day stripping boilers and dismantling the electrical switchboard bay and ferrying disused equipment from the vents to the sheds and stacking broken alternator laminator panels in a pile and a thousand other acts of regression it didn't take a genius to pull things apart but jeez it was depressing work.

—

At lunchtimes just to cheer themselves up yeah to keep themselves from going insane some bright spark brought in a couple of bikes and the men (because it was all men working there) yeah the men'd hold time trials around the compound.

There was a cooling water canal that ran round the perimeter of the yard all concrete and steel and barbed-wire fencing and alongside that canal ran a banked path like some grim Soviet velodrome. And when lunch rolled around everyone would down tools and pick up a bike but only when it was their turn oh there was an orderly system to it don't worry they'd have scratch races round the circuit on those two bikes yeah do laps wearing their yellow hard hats instead of helmets God they must've been desperate for fun. They all did it but not the foreman Sid said the foreman never joined in. Because he had enough fun busting everyone's balls all day long yeah that bloke's not short on entertainment Sid used to say that foreman was always frothing for a fight.

—

That's your scales of justice right there I told Sid. That's the universe's way of balancing out your good luck. I'd read all about it in *The Golden Treasury of Greek Mythology* I knew all about Nemesis the winged balancer of life.

Come again? Sid said.

It's the scales of justice you know the light and the dark the good and the bad.

Hippie s█ Sid said.

So I told Sid how Nemesis was the goddess of divine retribution and how she believed you shouldn't have too much of a good thing in your life so she cursed anyone whose life was too cruisey you know too blessed with good luck in order to balance the scales a bit.

But Sid said that was rubbish and good luck's there for the taking and what's it got to do with the foreman anyway?

He's the bad I said. The bad to balance out the fact that you and Chook are lucky enough to have jobs at all.

And I held my hands like scales: This one is your job and this one here is the foreman.

Ah but that's assuming a job's a good thing Sid said darkly think your scales might be a bit dodgy.

—

I believed it though I believed in divine retribution yeah I knew better than Sid on this one he was kidding himself if he couldn't see how the world worked: the bad with the good the yin with the yang a cloud for every silver lining.

Those scales they were always in balance for every good thing in life an equally bad thing was in the wings and boy did it pay to be ready yeah those scales of justice might've given me the heebie-jeebies but at least it meant I was prepared.

Oh I knew there was a method to the madness a pattern to the punches a kid knew what to expect in life and so you didn't go getting your hopes up too high when you knew you were due something bad.

—

Sid and Chook however were busy making their own stroke of luck *stroke of genius* if you asked them yeah the pair of them started bringing copper home from work scrap metal that they rescued from the bin.

Copper pipes copper cabling copper from overhead lights Sid ferried home copper wiring from electrical transformers copper tubing from heat exchangers once he salvaged a copper-mounted employee-of-the-month plaque – you can bet that plaque didn't say Sid's name.

Minding it for a mate was how Sid explained the copper. Just holding onto it for a bit.

And he did too. Chook might've transported it in the Sandman but it was Sid who stored all that copper at our house on Jabiru Avenue. All those rose-coloured wires all those black coils all those party-coloured plastic-coated cables lying on our lounge-room floor in bundles and piles and lazy figure eights or wound round crappy red reels it looked like a snake pit flipping Reptile Park there on the shagpile carpet. Yeah Sid held onto all that copper until he got the nod that is and then he and Chook would lug it back out to Chook's Sandman and drive it to the scrap yard on Wilga Road.

What do they do with it there I wanted to know.

And Sid would tap the side of his nose like he actually had a clue.

Then what if you go to all the trouble of getting it there and they don't need it and you don't get paid?

But Sid said there was no such thing as too much copper that they'd take everything he and Chook could bring.

Fine but what makes you think no one at the power plant notices when you waltz out the door with ten copper pipes tucked under your arm?

And that according to Sid was the smartest part of all oh they were working in cahoots with their boss that's right the foreman was taking a cut you've never heard anything so ■ing stupid the foreman was in on the whole thing.

Jesus why would you I said.

And Sid got all cryptic on me.

Keep your mates close and your enemies even closer he replied.

Like it was all part of some grand plan yeah like he and Chook weren't just sh■ scared of their boss.

—

Sid's first strike was beating the foreman in a time trial you know on the bikes at lunchtime by the canal. Like I said the foreman wasn't usually one to get stuck in but on this particular day he decided he'd have a go and Sid in his wisdom lined up to race against him.

A less honest bloke might've let his boss win. But not Sid and not that day oh no Sid was going for gold. The way Chook described it Sid almost set a new land-speed record around that canal yeah the foreman couldn't catch him for dust and the men cheered Sid's name and they banged their hard hats against the fence until those chain links almost broke apart. And the foreman flung his bike down and threw his hard hat to the ground with so much force that it split like a watermelon it was the foreman's first and last race and Sid was the one who beat him.

—

Sid's second mistake was hot chips if you really want to know. God it almost makes you laugh to think about it yeah it started with a carton of hot chips at work if only Sid had picked a pie.

It was a week or so after the bike race when Sid bought hot chips at lunchtime he was just about the last person in the canteen queue and when Narelle behind the counter saw Sid she blushed from the soles of her orthopaedic shoes to the tip of her canteen cap she gave him an extra-large scoop of hot chips leaving the bain-marie empty she threw in a free twenty-cent tomato sauce to boot.

So there's Sid sitting in the sun by the concrete canal seagulls circling the water sparkling through the chain-link fence and beside Sid is Chook and in between them stands the Mount Fuji of greasy hot chips. Yeah Sid's placed them there so Chook can partake too and they've squirted that tomato sauce on top and before he puts each chip in his mouth Sid swipes it through the tomato sauce first one side and then the next a single fluid movement like he's drawing infinity symbols like these are the magic pudding of chips yeah they might never run out.

Doggedly they ate.

But before they'd destroyed all the evidence a shadow fell across Sid and Chook and from where they were sitting that shadow's thicker than the power station's two chimneystacks combined and twice as ugly as well. It was the foreman and he's cracking the sh▮ts yeah he's screaming blue bloody murder because some mongrel bought the last of the hot chips and that mongrel looked a lot like Sid.

And the next thing Sid knew he was ten centimetres in the air which is a long way up when you consider Sid's starting from a decent vantage point what with him being so tall but the foreman had him by the shirtfront and he was swearing in Sid's face and worse he was spitting in the last of Sid's chips. Three strikes and you're out the foreman warned Sid before lowering him back to the ground and it might look like Sid's got a problem with authority but no. Authority's always had a beef with Sid.

—

By now Sid was firmly in the bad books with the foreman probably never in his good books to be honest and so Sid decided he'd try to atone why couldn't he lie low for once.

For months Sid had been bringing scrap metal home from work but now he stepped up his efforts oh he was going to make the foreman rich. The price of copper was sky high yeah copper was having its day in the sun worth its weight in gold Sid would tell me proudly and I didn't like to point out that was the wrong f▮▮▮▮g metal Sidney.

There was no shortage of scrap metal at Munmorah for all those months while they dismantled the joint but now Sid shifted things up a gear he and Chook were bringing home copper every second day. Once they swaggered home from the power station wearing sleeves of copper plumbing pipe on their arms for my benefit another time they stumbled in stiff-legged with sawn-off copper pipes swivelling round their skinny calves like Tin Man in *The Wizard of F█ing Oz*. Another time they came through the front door at Jabiru Avenue with twelve metres of copper cabling slung between them like a long looping python. They were crazy that night the pair of them were carrying on so much I figured they were drunk but then I worked out they were overexcited oh they were hyper as kids on cordial.

Copper load of this eh Red! Copper look! Geddit? C'mon copper look yeah cop a Captain Cook.

They dumped the cable ceremoniously at my feet which dangled off the end of the couch. Wow I said without looking up from my book you blokes need the whole drive down from San Remo to think up that one pun?

Aw don't be like that Ruby Tuesday they said c'mon have a look just have a look honestly they were like a pair of puppies they were practically begging for a pat.

Go on then what is it I said even though honestly it was better not to know.

It's the main line —

The number-one line —

Protection cabling —

To the switchyard —

They were tripping over each other in their excitement to tell me tripping over each other and tripping over the cable as well.

You'll bust it you d■heads.

We already have! they said and they cracked themselves up then yeah they just about wet themselves there on the shagpile plush the two of them yahooing and carrying on until I thought Chook might just lay an egg.

We tripped the transmission Chook said. And Sid said how the pair of them had taken down all 250 kV of transmission lines when they cut the cables yeah when they removed the protection cables running to Munmorah Switchyard and how they could've wiped out power to half the region and nearly wiped out themselves into the bargain.

You two'll get done for this I said with disgust.

Nah Sid said we're doing them a favour it was going to the dump anyway.

But Chook said: What arrested for misconduct geddit? Copper metal mis*conduct*!

And that set them off again they could barely stand up by then they were laughing so hard I told them to rack off I was trying to read. Go on I said *I'll Cu later* but they didn't get it yeah my periodic-table pun went straight over their heads and they went to sit out the back and crack a few beers and honestly I was working with amateurs.

—

The great copper escapade continued seamlessly for a spell Sid and Chook were regular little recyclers yeah proper little cogs in some larger machine they were rats running round their wheels they kept bringing home those copper cables and pipes from the increasingly derelict power station leaving the house each morning at sparrow's fart wandering out to the Sandman empty-handed and returning at night laden down and then when the time was right the pair of them offloaded the stuff at the scrap-metal yard on Wilga Road and then they delivered the proceeds to the foreman and it was all going swimmingly it was working like clockwork until everything went belly up.

—

Trouble arrived as it usually did when Sid went down to the track. It was there at Saratoga Racecourse between the end of race nine and a late scratching for race ten that Sid got talking to someone who could do him a better price on the catalytic converter that he and Chook brought home last Tuesday yeah a better price than the scrap-metal yard on Wilga Road was offering.

Deadset? I said to Sid half-heartedly because it was hard to get excited when you knew Sid's track record yeah Sid's record down at the track.

Sid was excited though. Sid with his eye for a bargain Sid who never had the sense to quit when he was ahead and not even when he was behind yeah Sid who couldn't have identified a bad idea if it facepalmed him square in the forehead. And so Sid went off and sold the catalytic converter to the guy from the racecourse instead of going with Chook to the usual joint up on Wilga Road and he made some good money more than they usually got and wouldn't the foreman be proud of him oh honestly Sid was a kid.

—

Not that I cared I had enough to worry about that particular week without keeping an eye on Sid's copper racket hell it were eyes that were causing all my problems that week yeah it were eyes that were giving me headaches.

We were doing eyes in science and especially the function of the cornea and so we had to dissect a cow's eye because they're very similar to human ones and because you can't buy a class set of human eyes at McGovern's Butchers and not even at Deepwater Plaza.

First step in dissecting a cow's eye is to use a scalpel to cut away all the excess fat and muscle tissue from the eyeball to remove the stuff around the optic nerve and I was doing this I was making a neat job of it too when Tamara Archer started giving sh█ to Stevie about being my lab partner but not wanting to touch the cow's eye. Got your b█tch doing your dirty work for you Tamara Archer was saying. What too chickensh█ to touch a cow Stevie. And Stevie ignored her because he was good like that but honestly it made me see red.

I was just up to the bit where you drain that putrid black liquid from the cow's eye when something slick and sloppy spitballed through the air it landed wetly on the side of Stevie's neck. And Stevie screamed and flicked that black glob to the floor but its goo still oozed down his collar. It was Tamara Archer she'd chucked the gunk from her cow's eye right at Stevie I didn't see the funny side myself.

No I didn't see the humour and I didn't stop to think either I scooped up my cow's eye it was half dissected one chunk dangling like a semi-sliced boiled egg I pegged it at Tamara Archer and it connected alright it hit her right by her mouth.

She squealed and Mr Hendricks our science teacher finally looked up from *The Hitchhiker's Guide to the Galaxy* and noticed what was going on he leaped off his lab stool and rushed over to Tamara Archer where that thing had landed so close to her mouth she could've stuck out her tongue and licked it.

—

Practically bullseye you'd say.

—

She called me a psycho. When Mr Hendricks led me outside she yelled psycho at my back even though she'd started it yeah I was just giving her a taste of her own medicine. But who cares let her be scared of me let them all be f■king afraid so what if they think I'm some kind of psycho so long as they leave Stevie alone. Anyway I was only getting wound up yeah plenty more where that came from I stopped off at McGovern's Butchers on the way home from school and I bought a pair of bull's testicles wrapped in a blue plastic butcher's bag yeah to put in Tamara Archer's locker.

—

I'd just got home that day just made myself a Milo sandwich with white bread margarine dry Milo powder plus two white sugars when somebody knocked at the door. Sid was still at work or at the White Hart or at the TAB most likely so when I answered the door and saw someone I didn't recognise I told him he was wasting his time.

He's not here I said.

He had these eyes these small piggy eyes they were almost swallowed up by his face his nose looked like it had lived more of its life busted than it ever sat straight and his skin was this awful mottled pink and pasty white in patches like it'd been burned or something. *Here* was a face like a kicked-in biscuit tin wait till Stevie heard about this.

I'll wait he said.

He put a fat fist against the doorframe and with the other hand he yanked the flyscreen so the door bounced open. He stepped inside the house and pushed past me and headed down the dark corridor he glanced into the lounge room where the blinds were pulled low and the lights were off it was in its usual pigsty state cables and plumbing pipes and cardboard boxes and a freaking shipping pallet propped against one wall and he decided against it yeah he kept walking he headed into the kitchen where an overhead light burned in spite of the blazing afternoon sun and my sandwich sat the Milo powder clumping the bread drying out in the heat.

I followed him into the kitchen.

On the kitchen windowsill there was a plain pine box stuffed full of envelopes it held bills first notices second notices final notices also notes sent home from school they sat in that box in the full glare of the sun until they yellowed like leaves on a vine.

Now this stranger stood in the middle of the kitchen and lit a cigarette he studied the lit end momentarily and then looked up and when he saw that pine box full of paperwork he upturned it on the kitchen bench. He began to sift through our old bills.

What the hell I said.

God where was Sid where was Chook where were any of them oh panic was rising in my throat our house was normally crawling with B Division Rovers and now that I needed them I was on my own. Sod's Law or Sid's Law more like it.

What do you want I said but my voice gave me away yeah the way it wobbled like that. Not that it mattered because he ignored me anyway I tried again tougher this time.

I'd offer to make you one I said. And I made a show of poking my sandwich I was right it was already going hard but then that bread was hardly fresh baked to begin with.

But I don't reckon you've dropped by for a Milo sandwich have you? I said.

And he grinned at that and called me a f[illegible]g smartarse but he didn't pause from sifting through those envelopes and one or two fluttered to the floor his cigarette hung precariously from the corner of his mouth his fingernails were black and stubby.

Who are you I said.

Who am I? He laughed. I'm the finance manager from Wilga Road.

He finished rifling through the letters then he swiped one hard arm across the bench sending papers flying and knocking the pine box onto the floor its cheap wood splintering along one side. Next he walked over to the dining-room table which was covered in junk – a box of fishing tackle a stack of old newspapers a hacksaw I wished Sid hadn't left in easy reach. My school bag was sitting on top of the newspapers and he picked it up its canvas straps undone its mouth flapping as he shook it upside down and *Signpost Maths* and a can of Impulse Free Spirit deodorant and a blue plastic butcher's bag holding two bull's testicles tumbled to the floor.

But none of those things were what he was after not the textbook not the Impulse and not the bull's balls. He kicked at the lot in frustration and walked into the lounge room I swiped the butcher's bag up off the floor it had another clear plastic bag inside it what you think I would carry a pair of balls without double-bagging them.

I followed him into the lounge room where he stood in the centre of the room and spun slowly his cigarette still hanging from his mouth he removed it with two thick fingers and ashed it in mid-air and little flecks of grey rained on the carpet.

Jesus he said how would you find anything in this sh█thole?

And I might've been absolutely packing s██ but I also knew just how he felt.

—

He stood like that surveying the mess and smoking his cigarette and ashing it on the shagpile and then something in him snapped and he stormed over to the packing pallet propped against the wall and pulled it and it came crashing down onto the coffee table clattering against the orange mosaic tiles of the tabletop and sending Sid's VB-can-ashtray flying.

Next he toed a stack of plumbing pipes lying on the carpet and the sound said he was wearing steel-capped boots. He crossed the room away from where I was flattened against the doorframe and he picked up Sid's armchair by its two spindly armrests he lifted it high into the air then he flung it at the wall and one skinny wooden leg kicked straight through the fibro that chair stayed stuck there pegged to the wall yeah reclining at a jaunty angle.

After that he gave up on the lounge room he thundered through the doorway on the far side and he crossed the hall. In my bedroom I could hear smashing swearing tinkle of glass I heard a grunt and a muffled thud – he must've upturned the mattress I don't know what it was he was looking for but he was fairly pissed off he couldn't find it.

I followed him as far as the corridor and stood in the sliced sunshine that streamed through the screen door in shafts.

He emerged from my bedroom then and went straight into Sid's room he ignored me standing there in the hallway and in Sid's room I could hear crashing cracking the terrifying whump of a toppled wardrobe.

Where the f▇▇ is it he roared coming out of Sid's room. I was still holding that butcher's bag I still had one finger looped through the thin plastic handles and I looked up at his mottled face all pink and patchy white and now also red with rage and I looked at his tiny squinting eyes his thick neck. I looked at him standing there in his navy collared shirt and his navy shorts and his steel-capped boots his hands making fists by his side and I don't know why but I said here it is and I held the plastic bag out to him.

He snatched the bag by its neck.

Then he yanked it open one flimsy handle in each hand and the blue plastic split and the clear plastic bag inside *that* split as well and two glistening pink testicles fell on the floor.

Those balls were pale smooth wrinkled delicately at each end. Bull's balls are big and each one McGovern's Butchers had given me was about the size of a small Frankfurt sausage but rounder more ball-shaped obviously. And if you squinted you could make out their marbled blue veins as they lay in that green shagpile paddock.

When they fell one of the balls had landed on his boot it bounced off the toecap and rolled onto the floor but not before it left a wet smudge on the leather. He looked at that smudge and he looked at those balls and then he put his fist through the fibro wall by my head.

I slid to the carpet my back pressed to the wall my legs concertinaing beneath me. I tucked my head under my arm and I waited for the blow to come but what arrived was Sid with good timing for once.

What the – Ruby! Sid said.

And he barrelled through the front door.

Sid launched himself at the pig-eyed man lowered his long neck and bulldozed into him head-on and when the pig-eyed man doubled over Sid stood up and delivered an uppercut to his jaw and the man's mouth snapped shut and his head snapped back and Sid looked like he didn't know what was more shocking the sound of his fist against somebody's jawbone or the fact that he'd connected at all.

Sid was a lover not a fighter he'd run a mile to avoid a brawl never kick a cow patty on a hot day he'd say when I came home from school and I'd split someone's lip now he'd gone and kicked that cow patty good and hard oh the ■ sure was hitting the fan.

The pig-eyed man staggered backwards he slumped into the corridor wall and Chook arrived then he'd been three or four steps behind Sid coming in from the car and now he appeared just in time to see the pig-eyed man steady himself against the wall he raised his head up and his pig-eyes were blazing and Chook shouted but it was too late and the pig-eyed man lumbered forward he swung and hit Sid above the cheekbone.

The pig-eyed man swayed with the effort of hitting Sid and when he found his balance he started moving forward again he pushed past me and past Sid who was doubled up on the carpet he was heading for Chook in the doorway.

—

Chook looked like a statue like a stocky garden gnome (Chook who was barely tall enough to reach the doorbell) yeah little Chook Fowler whose feathers I liked to ruffle by leaning down and messing up his hair.

Now though Chook stood there like he was ready for what was coming like he was daring this guy to have a go and at the very last second just as the pig-eyed man reached Chook and I thought we were off to his funeral yeah just as I was hailing a hearse Chook raised the arm that had been hidden behind the doorframe and he clobbered the pig-eyed man with an aluminium downpipe he sank like a sack of cement.

Jesus Chook where'd you pull that from I asked.

Number-four switchboard bay at work Chook said soberly.

He dropped the downpipe and it clattered onto the concrete step. In the doorway the pig-eyed man lay groaning and holding his head where the edge of the downpipe had collected him blood was pouring from a gash that was dangerously close to his temple and further along the hallway Sid was still out for the count.

Whaddawe do Chook?

And Chook stood in the doorway and surveyed the scene he looked from the pig-eyed man with blood running down his face and then over to Sid passed out yeah pale as a clean sheet. Then Chook's eyes fell on the patch of carpet in front of me.

Jesus Red he said in rising panic where's the bloke that's lost *those* balls?

—

Chook and I weaponed up. He armed himself with his aluminium downpipe again while I went and got the hacksaw from the dining-room table I'd never used a hacksaw before didn't know how but the pig-eyed man didn't need to know that did he I was a girl that carried around sawn-off balls after all.

Right said Chook when I returned with my hacksaw.

He kicked the pig-eyed man in the guts.

Who are you and what do you want Chook said to him but the man just groaned he was curled up in a small 'c'.

Chook kicked him again.

He was holding the downpipe above his waist like a cricket bat like he was about to hit the best pull shot the Yattalunga B Division Rovers had ever seen yeah if this bloke didn't hurry up with a good answer Chook was ready to hit him for six.

Then just as the pig-eyed man opened his mouth to speak and just as Chook looked ready to swing wouldn't you know it Sid woke up and vomited violently.

Quick Red we need to roll him over Chook instructed as Sid began to choke on his own chunder.

So Chook took his shoulders while I gripped his hips and between the two of us we managed to roll the whole lanky length of Sid onto his side. He coughed and spluttered worse than the Sandman on a cold morning and then he was sick all over again but after that the life seemed to flood back into him and he focused on us for the first time.

Ruby he said. Rube are you —

He tried to sit up but his head had other ideas and he collapsed back onto the carpet and moaned.

Easy tiger said Chook. You're looking worse than usual mate.

I wiped Sid's mouth with the back of my hand and he grimaced with pale shaky lips.

Ruby Tuesday he said.

His cheekbone where the pig-eyed man had punched him was swelling fast turning red-purple angry. It was stretched and taut where a lump was growing.

I'll get something for your face I said.

And I went to stand up but then Chook shouted Stop! And I froze on the spot and I stayed there crouched down alongside Sid. And when I half turned my head I saw the pig-eyed man stumbling out the front door bleeding as he ran across the lawn past the empty ornamental pond where the gnome just stood dumbly and let him get away and I understood Chook hadn't meant me.

We should go after him!

He's all yours said Chook and he rocked back on his heels.

The two of us were still squatting by Sid's side Chook on the right and me on the left with Sid between us looking like death warmed up.

Who the hell was he anyway Chook asked.

You tell me I said. He came here looking for something.

And I thought about the upturned pine box and the scattered paperwork in the kitchen how he'd called himself the finance manager.

He was looking for cash I told them.

Cash? Chook repeated.

Sid said: Did you tell him he got the wrong address.

I'm gunna get you something for your face I replied.

—

In the kitchen I opened the freezer and pulled out a bag of frozen peas it was that or one of four frozen meat pies that were rattling around in there. The lino was still littered with the bills and final notices that had pinwheeled to the floor earlier. In the dining room *Signpost Maths* lay splayed on the floorboards while my can of Impulse had rolled under the table and out the other side and had finished up in the dust balls along the skirting.

I walked back to Sid and Chook in the corridor.

He came from Wilga Road I said remembering.

Chook was standing now my hammies he complained and he rubbed his hamstrings ruefully he'd stayed squatted beside Sid for too long.

He nodded at the bull's testicles on the carpet.

And what about the balls where'd they come from.

But Sid said: Wilga Road? You sure about that?

From the scrap yard you mean? Chook asked.

Dunno. He never told me I said.

Chook's eyes narrowed suspiciously.

Why would a bloke from Wilga Road come visiting said Chook. You been out to the scrap yard recently.

But Sid hadn't been out to the Wilga Road scrap yard recently not yesterday and not the day before and not even the day before that when he was supposed to go out there with the catalytic converter that he and Chook brought home from work. Sid never delivered the catalytic converter like they'd arranged. Instead he'd sold it to the guy he got talking to at Saratoga Racecourse on Saturday morning and he hadn't thought to mention that fact to Chook.

I got a better price for it Sid said.

You got a better price for it Chook said slowly.

Chook turned away from Sid then and raised his arms to the ceiling and the movement made a Celtic-knot tattoo poke out from his navy shirtsleeve. In my hand the frozen peas were starting to sting my fingers I held them out and Sid took the bag without a sound and he pressed it gingerly to his head and then Chook exhaled and when he turned towards us again all the colour had drained from his face.

Jesus Sidney do you know what you've done do you have any idea what you've gone and done Chook said.

I – Chooky I was just trying to get us a better price. Chook? Chook I was just trying to —

Jesus Christ Sidney!

And Sid was scrambling now he propped himself up on one elbow and turned awkwardly to face Chook while the other hand still held half a kilo of No Name baby peas to his head.

It was a better price Chook a better price he kept saying.

F▇▇ the price Sid! We're f▇ked. Oh f▇▇ we're f▇▇ed we're really royally f▇▇ed.

Somewhere inside me something sank.

But how did the scrap yard on Wilga Road know you'd used a different buyer I asked and why would they send someone round to collect the money? Why would they think they were owed anything it didn't make any sense.

Have you heard of Operation Igneous Sid? Chook said ignoring me.

Sid hadn't.

Operation Igneous Chook said is how four blokes got arrested in possession of two thousand dollars' worth of copper from Gosford train station last month while we can bring home all the copper and aluminium and whatever the ▇▇ we like from the Munmora Power Station without anyone raising an eyebrow. Operation Igneous Sidney is how those blokes are now looking at prison time while you and I keep delivering a tidy profit to the foreman *so long as we sell our stuff at the scrap-metal yard on Wilga Road!*

Chook was shouting now.

Operation Igneous you d█head is the reason you and I can go about our business without the cops sticking their noses in did you ever consider that Sidney did you did you? Did you ever think about the fact the pigs never come sniffing around? Or what about the fact that no one at the scrap yard ever asks us where we get our stuff from no nobody ever gets suss about our never-ending supply nobody ever pays us the blindest bit of attention. How many blokes do you know with an unlimited supply of legal scrap metal Sidney how many blokes carry a catalytic converter in their back pocket? The cops leave us alone because of *the laugh* you know a retainer Sidney they're being paid to turn a blind eye!

Chook stopped shouting then and he walked over to Sid and stood with his feet apart and his fists on his hips and looked down at Sid's sorry face.

It's a police-sanctioned operation said Chook. At least it was until you buggered it up. So long as we sell our stuff to the scrap yard on Wilga Road then the cops will keep getting their cut.

It took a moment for the gravity of Chook's words to sink in yeah for Sid to consider their weight and when the reality of the situation hit home in Sid's head he turned politely away from Chook and he vomited on the shagpile again.

—

The next few days were tense alright Sid was a cat on a hot tin frigging roof while we waited for the cops to make their move while we waited for the axe to fall.

Chook took off for forty-eight hours we didn't see him or his Sandman for dust. He blamed Sid for going behind his back and selling to someone other than the Wilga Road scrap yard and Sid blamed Chook for not telling him he couldn't and Chook blamed Sid for receiving cash for the catalytic converter without Chook being present for the negotiations and Sid blamed Chook for getting him tangled up in a f■■ing police scam to begin with.

Somehow Sid's Mendini violin had survived the raid by the pig-eyed debt collector from Wilga Road. Sid's wardrobe door was unhinged and his mattress was slashed his armchair was marooned in the lounge-room wall and yet his violin stayed safe shoved under Sid's bed alongside his best lead fishing sinkers and his *Penthouse* magazine Christmas editions that's right Sid kept his Mendini and his tackle and his porn mags side by side all of Sid's valuables lived down there.

Now though Sid dragged that Mendini out he wandered round the house fiddling forlornly he walked laps of that circuit from the kitchen to the dining room to the lounge room to the hallway and back into the kitchen again he played fugues and requiems he moped with a face like a smacked arse. One afternoon he went and installed three new locks on the front door as if that might keep out what was coming as if that could hold back the tide.

Stevie and I stayed out of his way when he was in this mood there was no point trying to talk to Sid when he was flat out feeling sorry for himself.

No we'd sit down at the wharf or on this day just on the back steps and watch the sunset as the sky turned from gold to bronze to gobsmacking pink we'd sniff the salt coming in off the bay. A colony of flying foxes was nursing nearby and every day at dusk those bats would rise up like a plume of black smoke they'd spread out they'd disperse squealing and screeching pinpricking the sky from a distance they looked like beautiful black birds it was only up close you could see they had teeth.

I read this thing Stevie said. Where if you join a band you arrest development at whatever age you were when you joined.

He sat sideways on the concrete step with his back resting against the upright post of the handrail and his head against the horizontal bar his body was turned towards me but his face was tipped to the sky.

Arrest development I parroted. That's deep. What does it mean like you don't grow up? Jesus every man in Australia must've been in a band at some point.

Ha ha Stevie said.

That'd be a good name for a band I said. Arrested Development.

Arresting An Elephant he joked.

A Red-handed Elephant.

No a Red-*headed* Elephant! he replied he scratched his chin thoughtfully.

The Pestilent Redheads he said after a while. Now there's a name for a band.

The Eminent Redheads. Malevolent Redheads?

The Malevolent Redheads yeah that sounds about right said Stevie. Tamara Archer would agree with that.

Because it was true I'd left those bull's balls in her locker and she'd screamed the place down when she found them yeah when she'd discovered them all smooth and warm and starting to smell yeah wrapped in her clean PE t-shirt.

She had it coming I said. I know what about Petulant Celibate?

Did Tamara Archer make you think of that Stevie said and I smirked.

Decadent Pessimist? Negligible Benefit?

Hesitant Embezzlement said Stevie.

Yeah I *like* it that's my band name now: Hesitant Embezzlement. Where'd you learn that thing about arrested development anyway I said. You didn't read that in *TV Hits* did you.

No he admitted I read it in one of Mum's magazines.

Because Stevie's mum was always reading about personal growth and the power of teen esteem yeah Mrs Madigan was an armchair expert when it came to parenting teenagers.

So like Michael Hutchence will always be seventeen years old even when he's a pensioner?

Yeah Stevie said. I mean if that's how old he was when they formed INXS then yeah I guess inside he'll always be seventeen.

And it was funny but I couldn't imagine Michael Hutchence getting old like it sort of made sense that he'd stay young yeah inevitable in a rockstar kinda way.

What about Axl Rose how old was he when he joined Guns N' Roses I asked.

Dunno early twenties maybe.

And Angus Young how old was he when they formed Acca Dacca?

Who do I look like Molly Meldrum jeez Red I dunno.

And I laughed and stretched luxuriously towards the sky because it was so easy to make Stevie exasperated but it never stopped being funny.

Above me a she-oak drooped its branches were shaggy and turning rusty brown at the tips each branch made up of clumps like tiny brushes and I tore one of the brushes off and twirled it between my fingers a bouquet of dry pine needles.

He was supposed to come here don't you know said Stevie.

Who Molly Meldrum.

Angus Young said Stevie. He was booked to play this one time at Frogy's but he never showed up.

And it was no lie that Frogy's roller-skating rink sometimes had live music but the Angus Young part sounded far-fetched even for Stevie.

Imagine if you could choose what age to stay at I said.

Like by joining a band you mean.

No dumb█se without joining a band I said. Like just press pause and stay at one age forever.

I picked the small hard catkins off my branch and pegged them at Stevie one by one hitting his shoulder his arm bouncing one off his forehead.

Like imagine if you could just choose I said. I'd be twenty-six yeah that's when I'd stop the clock I want to be twenty-six forever.

You don't even know what twenty-six will be like.

Twenty-six will be awesome.

I flicked my whole bouquet at Stevie then but he caught it easily and then he sat and pulled a pine needle off and snapped it methodically at each segment. The wind was picking up it moaned in the trees the sun had set while we were sitting out there and the world was grey again.

Do you think there's a chance the cops might just drop it Stevie said after a while.

Mmm don't reckon that's their style I said.

I pictured Sid's Datsun all those years ago yeah the way it looked with all four doors smashed in and the windscreen shattered how it sagged with its bonnet bashed and how Sid had sagged too.

They'll show up I said. Any day now.

I drew my legs up to my chest folded them like freckly flamingo legs I picked at the scabs on my knees.

So why don't you take off for a few weeks Stevie wanted to know. You and Sid just the two of you or Chook as well if he wanted yeah you could head up the coast for a bit and then come back when everything's cooled off —

He stopped when he saw the look on my face.

Why should we? I said.

And even I was surprised by the fury in my voice but really why should we be the ones to leave. Because despite it all yeah despite everything that Jabiru Avenue *wasn't* – and believe me the list was long – it was our place sure it was hardly blue-chip real estate what with its besser-block letterbox and its paint-chipped garden gnome its carport corroding in the sun. No not that flash with its rusting fridge carcass out the back and its empty carp pond out the front and its junk-filled full-to-the-gills weatherboard house in between but despite that yeah despite it all Jabiru Avenue was our place it was mine and Sid's so why should we be the ones to leave.

Stevie shrugged.

It's your funeral he said.

But he wouldn't meet my eye when he said it so I knew he wasn't as cool about it as he was trying to make out. He was still holding the branch I threw at him and now he swept it absent-mindedly back and forth across the concrete step between us as if he could sweep away our conversation. Then he plucked the one green needle off the branch and stuck it in the corner of his mouth he chewed it thoughtfully while he stared out across the backyard and while we waited for the stars to appear.

I'd choose now you know Stevie said out of the blue.

For what?

You know like you said before. If you could press pause and stay any age I'd choose now I'd stay like this right here.

—

Sergeant Healy was an all-encompassing but weirdly invisible presence for so much of my childhood in the same way other kids have Jesus or Santa or I don't know what yeah I had the threat of Sergeant Healy hanging over my head only you don't want him ho-ho-hoing down your chimney no the sarge sure as hell weren't no lamb of God.

I'd never seen Sergeant Healy had never laid eyes on him and I always sort of thought I must've overinflated him in my imagination you know that I'd got sucked in by Sid's stories and I'd turned Healy into some monster that was way more menacing than was ever possible and that one day I'd see him and he'd just be this short-arsed cop with a big gun and a tiny ████ yeah real Napoleon syndrome.

A small ████ walking around on short stocky legs that's what I expected Healy to be. So you can understand why I was caught off-guard when he turned up looking like a Grimms' fairytale giant yeah like David's f████ing Goliath.

His feet were long in shiny black shoes and I wondered stupidly where you bought shoes so big. It was obscenely hot that afternoon but Sergeant Healy was immaculately dressed in black slacks and a white collared shirt there was no incriminating police uniform no the sergeant's visit was strictly social. He seemed entirely relaxed about finding himself on our pink concrete doorstep as if that too belonged to him his eyes were the coldest blue stones you've ever seen.

His hair was blond and combed over and it looked recently wet as if he'd gone to the trouble of showering before he paid us a visit but the look on his face said make no mistake he'd be showering again afterwards.

He filled the doorway darkly. Both arms braced against the frame. And where the sun streamed through at the slim edges of his silhouette he became an inkblot test.

Who the – I started to say.

But Healy held his index finger towards my moving lips taking care not to actually touch them and my words just evaporated in the heat. I backed away from his hand and he stepped forward at the same time like the two of us were attached by the same short length of rope.

Our house seemed to shrink with Sergeant Healy inside it. Each box each crate each copper pipe even the chicken coop in the lounge room it all shrivelled down to doll's-house size when Healy walked past it. He walked calmly methodically down the corridor through the lounge room and out into the dining room where Sid sat among the rubble at the dining-room table reading the form guide and rolling fishing sinkers from squares of lead that were the size of a postage stamp and when Sid saw the sergeant he put down his long-nosed pliers and dropped his tiny lead square his face was as grey as his sinkers.

Sergeant Healy … I can … Sid said and he started rising out of his seat.

And Sergeant Healy laughed and the sound made Sid slump back down in his chair just like it made the bottom of my stomach drop away. So Sid knew the sergeant (even if I'd never laid eyes on him) and the sergeant sure as hell knew Sidney.

It's about the catalytic converter isn't it about the copper and the catalytic converter and I didn't know the place out on Wilga Road was your joint – Chook and I were just – we didn't know said Sid.

And while Sid talked I walked in the opposite direction around the loop to Healy yeah I went into the kitchen where the fridge hummed self-distractedly in the corner a bag of frozen prawns slowly softened in the sink. I went to the cutlery drawer and pulled it open it groaned on its wooden runners and I swore under my breath but then I took out a boning knife that was old and pretty blunt Sid had a better one but this one would do the job if it came to it whatever that job might be I didn't seriously think I'd actually use it but

I wrapped that knife in the hem of my t-shirt anyway all the while keeping my eyes on the sergeant through the doorway to the dining room.

Sergeant Healy stood facing Sid and he unbuttoned his shirt cuffs carefully and smoothed down the fabric of his wide-collared shirt then he rolled up each meticulous white sleeve. He had just removed his watch and placed it on the dining-room table among Sid's sinkers and the cracked tackle box and the newspaper open at the trots when the front flyscreen door banged open and in shuffled Chook.

Chook's head hung down his work shirt was ripped so that one short navy sleeve swung free meanwhile he was handcuffed and trailed by two pigs in blue that's right two of New South Wales Police Service's finest followed Chook in through the door.

Have you ever heard – Healy spoke directly to Sid without acknowledging Chook or the police officers who shoved Chook into the dining room ahead of themselves – about the man who used to eat his lunch underneath the Eiffel Tower?

Healy was strangely soft spoken for such a big man his voice was whisky on ice.

This man Healy said he ate his lunch there every day even though he hated that tower he thought it was the ugliest thing ever built in Paris. Do you know why?

But Sid didn't know why and he shook his head miserably.

He sat there Sidney at the foot of the Eiffel Tower because that was the only place in the whole of the f■■ing city where he couldn't see that f■■ing tower.

Sergeant Healy laughed to himself and then stopped abruptly.

That's why I like coming here Sidney he said. I like visiting your little house here on Jabiru Avenue I like coming here because when I'm inside your house and I'm talking to you Sidney it saves me having to see this █████ eyesore from the street.

In the kitchen I squeezed my fist tighter around the knife handle the hem of my tee growing damp I didn't know he'd been in our house before I'd never seen him there. Meanwhile in the dining room Sergeant Healy hadn't finished with his lectures for today he was just getting started so it seemed.

Now do you know about the broken-windows theory of policing said Healy. Of course you don't you █████ idiot let me tell you about it.

And while I stood gripping my knife and Sid sat pale-faced at the dining-room table surrounded by sinkers and boxes and the spread-out sports section Sergeant Healy told us how criminals like us see a rundown house with broken windows and an overgrown yard and we see an opportunity.

That's right an opportunity he said.

A chance to sell drugs or strip cars or bang prostitutes or bash our wives or whatever else we were into oh yeah apparently it was a known fact that a dump like ours was a sign a signal that the rats had moved in and taken over a broken window wasn't just a broken window it was a sign of weak social control that's why it was up to Sergeant Healy to come around every so often and clear us rats out yeah it was his job to fumigate.

Why don't you just fix the █████ windows for us? Chook said.

But the cop standing next to Chook didn't like that no he didn't like that one bit and he bent Chook forward so his handcuffed wrists were raised high behind him and then he ploughed him headfirst into the door frame.

Chook went down.

From where I stood in the kitchen I couldn't see Chook where he landed so I couldn't tell if he was conscious or not all I knew was he was pretty quiet after that yeah he didn't contribute too much to the conversation.

Perhaps you can assist us with our inquiries Sidney. Healy's voice was dangerously quiet he smirked each time he said 'Sidney' like even Sid's name was a joke.

Sid eyed him warily and rightly so I watched as Healy walked over to the phone on the wall its coiled cord in a cream-coloured knot. On the floor below the knot was a stack of sunny yellow phone books most of them still in their original plastic wrapping though the one Sergeant Healy picked up off the stack had been freed and he flipped the pages with one oversized thumb just to show how thick that thing was.

No – said Sid because he'd seen what was coming but the sergeant ignored him and went and belted Sid across the head with one-and-a-half kilos of L–Z.

You've always been a fly in my ointment Sidney.

And he hit Sid in the head again with the phone book where it left no mark that's right there was no point of impact that was the whole intention.

A pest. *Whack.*

Did you know that Sidney. *Whack.*

You're a pest. *Whack.*

The sort of pest that needs fumigating. *Whack.*

You've always been a pest. But now you're turning out to be a real ball-ache for me. *Whack.*

And Sid's head lolled backwards he gripped the edge of the table a lone lead fishing sinker rolled onto the floor and Sergeant Healy kicked it away with the toe of his boot so it ricocheted off the skirting board.

What did you think you were doing selling a stolen catalytic converter to the wrong receiver Healy said. It's not all beer and skittles running a copper racket Sidney but you never stopped to think about that did you Sidney no you never stopped to think about it from my point of view did you. You never stop to think at all do you Sidney.

Sergeant Healy didn't even bother to try to hide his disgust he spat the words out with revulsion.

You're a dream out walking Sidney. You're piss-weak and you're a dreamer.

It sounded like it was just about the worst insult he could come up with each syllable laced with loathing.

Didn't you wonder how you were getting away with it for so long Sidney? What did you think you and Fowler here had come up with something clever said Healy did you think you'd worked something out for yourselves.

He hit Sid again and the sound was sickening and Sid's eyes were rolling back in his head.

You broke the rules Sidney. You broke the rules and you went off on your own and now what am I going to do with you.

Sid was protesting now he wasn't above grovelling he didn't know he was breaking the rules couldn't possibly have known and it wouldn't happen again he could promise.

But the sergeant was saying too right it wouldn't happen again.

You're mine now Healy said. You're mine do you see that Sidney?

And I watched from the kitchen as he hit Sid one more almighty time with the phone book and the t-shirt in my hand was wet with sweat and the knife inside my t-shirt was damp too and I watched as that cop threw the literal f██king book at Sid and I got what it was to feel rage.

Sergeant Healy turned side-on then and let the phone book fall to the floor.

What do you want asked Sid.

You're up sh█ creek barked Healy. The best thing you can do is start paddling. You hear me! Start paddling Sidney!

The sergeant was growing expansive now he put his thumbs through his belt loops and arched his back.

Because you don't want one of my good officers here to have to load you up do you Sidney be a real pity if you got bricked up. Three grams of smack would be deemed supply that's trafficking territory a bloke could get put away.

I'd tell!

I never meant to speak but the words were out of my mouth before I could swallow them back down.

You'd tell? repeated Healy.

But he said it without bothering to turn and look at me instead he addressed his amusement at Sid as if it was Sid who'd spoken and not me from the kitchen yeah like I had no voice at all.

But who would you tell Sidney? And who are they going to believe? Me: the sergeant with the Commendation for Brave Conduct Sidney! Or a dopey bastard like you?

And the grim reality of his situation settled on Sid like a crow he lowered his head and stared at the table and shadow obscured his face.

Or said Healy as if the idea had just occurred to him. Or maybe you're prepared to testify against your mate Fowler here? What do you think have you got it in you Sidney just one little lie just a quick porky pie have you got it in you? You do!

Sergeant Healy's eyes lit up.

You'd rat on Fowler wouldn't you Sidney. Say it say it you dog say you'd rat on your mate you would wouldn't you – you know you would that is a dog act right there!

And I promise you Sid was just thinking of me when he dropped Chook right in it why else would he agree. Oh he said he was prepared to testify that the whole copper thing was Chook's idea. He was thinking of me and of how he could protect me but that doesn't mean that I had to like it oh I thought I'd be sick in the sink.

That's it then Sid said I'm free now aren't I.

Only Sergeant Healy didn't think so.

What whined Sid. I've given you blokes what you came here for so why can't you just piss off.

And my shame flickered and twisted and seemed to fill up the entire room until everything had the singed smell of disgrace it was my fault Sid did that to Chook.

—

Sergeant Healy warmed up his jaw then and when he spoke it was deliberate and slow as if he was speaking to a little kid oh I bet he talked down to his wife.

We're not even close to being done yet Sidney he said. What you've given us there is a little rainy-day investment a little something to keep up our sleeves but if I'm honest with you Sidney a notebook confession like that well … we would've come up with it ourselves.

What just make it up?

Look at that boys who says you can't teach an old dog new tricks! But we don't like to say *make it up* it's so crass don't you think.

But if Sid did think so then he didn't say.

No I'm afraid said Healy that it'll take more than that Sidney.

It will?

Sid was sounding tired now.

It will Sergeant Healy confirmed. Let me tell you about an operation that's being carried out by the boys over in the Transit Unit where they're taking in mongrels like you for copper thefts from State Rail.

Operation Igneous I said from the kitchen because I remembered Chook told us about it.

And Sergeant Healy's head whipped around and his eyebrows shot up oh I'd thrown him just for a second. Operation Igneous he confirmed and then he turned back to Sid.

Four blokes went down last month Sidney for trying to offload less than you and your mate Fowler have been shifting and now those four blokes are staring down the barrel of two years non-parole be a shame if you got caught up in all that Sidney be a real crying shame so what I'm proposing instead is that you keep your head down and do exactly as I say that's right you do a little bit of work for me and maybe you can avoid any nastiness – do you catch my drift are you with me Sidney are you getting all this.

And Sid was getting it all Jesus Christ he didn't need to be asked twice. Carry out a few jobs for the sergeant in exchange for avoiding arrest Sid couldn't sign up fast enough.

And Chook? Sid finally found the decency to ask. Is Chook part of this too?

Sergeant Healy looked amused at Sid's late loyalty still it suited him to use Chook too.

I like your enthusiasm Sidney he said. Who knew you had such a work ethic.

And then that was it the sergeant and his mates were leaving just like that. Sergeant Healy was picking up his watch from the dining-room table and dusting it off like it'd been contaminated sitting there among Sid's sinkers and he's putting it back onto his wrist and rolling down his sleeves again he's telling Sid to sit tight that the cops will contact him and Chook when they need them when they have a job for them and then he's smirking and asking Sid how it feels to be running with the big boys yeah how it feels to be playing first grade he has high hopes for their professional association he's saying then the three of them are swanning out the front door and Sid's still sitting at the dining-room table with his head buried in his shaky hands.

—

And Chook chose that moment to wake up he moaned and fumbled around on the floor frantic until he looked up and saw Sid then he calmed down he sat back against the wall.

They gone? What'd I miss mate? Chook asked.

Nothing pretty said Sid.

Jesus what happened to your head.

Not looking so flash yourself.

Nothing a bit of WD-40 won't fix Chook replied and he tried laughing but the movement made him groan loudly while in the kitchen I unrolled my damp t-shirt and slipped Sid's backup boning knife into the drawer.

—

So that's how we learned about the *green light* about the police party trick of granting permission yeah giving the signal. We learned there were police-sanctioned hold-ups and drug deals and gaming rackets and whatever you liked so long as the cops got a cut.

And that was just the tip of the iceberg yeah that was the bit we could see. I never knew it that day that Sergeant Healy came calling but those cops have their fingers in so many pies it's a miracle they have any fingers left over to scratch their police service ar█s.

I'm talking about theft and extortion and planting evidence and gratuities about improper associations with crims. About posing as a solicitor and advising suspects to cooperate with the cops even though it's not in the suspect's interests. About verballing suspects and unsigned records of interviews. About tampering with evidence and planting evidence about *scrumdowns* where they all get together and refresh one another's memories about an arrest they've made oh to ensure they're all telling the same lies. About offering false inducements to a suspect before an interview and then later denying all knowledge. About influencing criminal informants. About prior warning of police raids for their mates. And about *show raids* where nothing is searched and no one is arrested and then about lying under oath at committals about the operation. About revising police statements to destroy Crown cases in return for cash in their navy-blue pockets. About perjury process corruption about fraudulent practices. About protection of drug traffickers and gaming operators and pimps. About tow-truck rackets and spotters' fees for funeral-parlour operators. About interference with internal investigations about the code of silence about weeding out cops who are straight. About drinking on duty and drinking while driving and drinking while handling firearms. About threatening and abusing conduct. About assaults in custody about stalking and unlawful detention. Jeez even about the trading of winning TAB tickets to launder the proceeds of crime so that the person presenting the winning ticket at the counter wasn't the same bloke who bet on the horse seriously no institution was safe.

—

Stevie told me that just the other day they arrested a cop down in Sydney. They brought him in for falsely reporting the theft of his car the truth is he drove it into a pole on his way home from the pub where he was drinking with his cop mates. But once they started digging around they discovered he'd been involved in salting exhibits. That's right on his watch bank notes that were intended for an undercover police drug buy were planted at an accused's address meanwhile ground-up heroin that was confiscated from one premises was sprinkled under a table and along the edge of a knife somewhere else and then used as evidence at trial. Not to mention stealing money receiving bribes receiving payoffs and supplying seized drugs to informants the list was longer than your arm yeah that false car-theft report of his was just the tip of the iceberg that I was talking about and even though this story came from Stevie's mouth if even half of it's true that's bad enough.

—

I saw this documentary once about cops in New York City during the 1970s yeah before the Knapp Royal Commission drove a broom through the place this was in the bad old days at a time when they still called them *meat eaters* and *grass eaters*. The meat eaters were the ones like Sergeant Healy who went around establishing sophisticated payoff systems yeah the meat eaters made things happen. They were the ones who fabricated confessions who loaded up suspects with stolen gear it was the meat eaters who traded in seized firearms and confiscated drug hauls and who firebombed your car if you didn't play along. Yeah the meat eaters like Healy went out looking for it meanwhile the grass eaters were the cops that took what they found in their path.

And if it all went to sh█ yeah if things hit the fan then they'd simply claim *Hurt on Duty* entitlements and walk away with their police mates corroborating their story and a police pension in their pocket oh the system might've been stacked against people like us but it never failed insiders like them.

And it was a closed system it was a shut shop it was impenetrable to us. Justice was kept inside locked away safe from the touch of our grubby fingers it was the preserve of the cops and their mates yeah there might have been a whole galaxy of sanctioned corruption out there – a whole Milky Way of crooked cops of law enforcers who failed to enforce any laws and a justice department that turned a blind eye – but in that whole sprawling galaxy of crime by consent Sid was only one tiny pinprick star.

—

They call it the rotten-apple theory and the newspapers are full of it lately. How it's just one cop acting alone yeah one lone wolf. One rotten apple that's spoiling the barrel. As if there's not just rampant corruption like the whole force isn't rotten to the core.

—

I heard this thing on the radio about frozen apples once this was in Michigan. Ghost apples they called them it happens during cold snaps when freezing rain falls on the fruit trees and ices over the apples like the most perfect pane of glass you've ever seen. And because apples have a lower freezing point than water when the weather warms up those apples defrost faster than the ice encasing them and so those apples rot and slither out the bottom leaving the ice coating intact yeah leaving ghost apples hanging on the tree.

The New South Wales Police Service is full of ghosts just like that. The ghost of justice ghost of fairness like the Ghosts of f█ing Christmas Past. You won't find those things at Wyoming Police Station no way. No justice no fairness and you know what else you won't find? You won't find many good apples either.

—

Things took a bad turn after Sergeant Healy showed up at our joint and it didn't take a genius to see that. Sid and Chook began to do small jobs for the sergeant making deliveries accepting packages they were the fall guys who held the money or drugs from Healy's deals until he sent some of his men out to collect it.

It wasn't complicated work but it was risky as hell and even though I was sick to my stomach when I thought about what they were doing some small part of me was relieved as well because running with the cops wasn't like shifting copper or trading in second-hand whitegoods no it wasn't the sort of lifestyle that was sustainable for long and so whatever was coming our way was picking up speed oh it was really flying now it was hurtling towards us like a BMX down Jabiru Avenue.

The way I saw it our association with Sergeant Healy would be ancient history soon.

—

I read a lot during those days. I lay on the couch in the lounge room surrounded by a stack of boxed cordless drills and about a billion other things as well I lay there and I propped *The Golden Treasury of Greek Mythology* open against my ribs and I liked the weight of it there its green edge pressing against my bones I liked the way it reared and retreated with my breath.

Yeah I read with that book on my chest read all about scales and weighing. About Nemesis weighing up the good and the bad on those scales of hers about Zeus weighing the Keres of Achilles and Hector like he was spooning out doom oh I sat around with the weight of that book on my chest and the weight of the world on my shoulders.

—

Funny I'd thought the foreman back at Munmorah Power Station was our bad karma to balance how lucky Sid was to get a job. You know for every good thing an equally bad thing was coming. But now I could see I was wrong that I'd underestimated what it'd meant for Sid and Chook for all those blokes working out at Munmorah to have a job who cares that it was short-term work yeah that it was glorified destruction there was dignity in it (plus the paycheque didn't hurt). I saw that now. Just like I understood it was going to take something bigger uglier something more f█ed-up than the foreman to even the score yeah something in the form of Sergeant Healy to properly tip the scales.

Sergeant Healy who'd grown up with so much bile and hatred for us McCoys I couldn't imagine what it was like to live like that at least I couldn't until that rabid dog Healy showed up at our place yeah until he came and infected me with his hate all I've got now is hatred for him.

I hate what he made my dad do hate what he did to us and so I've become one of those winged Keres one of those watercolour monsters straight from the pages of my book ready to wreak havoc to wreak vengeance yeah I'm the black fate I'm death warmed up because that's the other thing: they reckon revenge is a dish best served cold but they're wrong it tastes good piping hot.

—

McCoy means *fire*. I know because we had a laminated poster stuck to the back of the toilet door so you could sit and do your business and contemplate the world while you learned the origins of our name. *McCoy pronounced: \me-'koi Origin: Irish Scottish and Manx developed from the Old Gaelic Mac Aodha.*

Whatever it's a Celtic pagan god and it means fire it means things are gunna burn.

(Specifically it means *son of fire* but you can bet that was written by a man.)

—

What smells like fish and rhymes with runt? Have you heard that one before.

Don't be so filthy the answer's: Rex Hunt.

—

But jeez that Sergeant Healy's a real Rex Hunt.

—

Yeah Sid and Chook were consorting with Sergeant Healy and by consorting I mean Healy had them by the balls. No wonder Sid was always in a foul mood when he got home from doing a job oh he was flipping filthy.

Once when he got back from wherever he'd been he had dark rings under his eyes and dark patches under his armpits and he was straight into the kitchen for a drink.

Not a good day to be a beer he said opening the fridge.

Then he swore and pounded the fridge he sounded disgusted as if it was me that had drunk all the tinnies.

I listened to him storm around the kitchen shoving drawers rattling cutlery like spare parts he went out the back door and then he came back in.

Geddoff your high horse and drink water I called. He hated it when I used his own words against him.

Always drink upstream from the herd I yelled.

Shut up he warned me from the kitchen. He'd been drinking already then.

After a while he appeared in the lounge room out of the corner of my eye I could see the saloon doors still swinging he went and stood between me and the TV screen and he palmed a hand across his scalp.

There's nothing in the freezer for tea he said forlornly honestly he was worse than a kid.

So go and get something I said.

I craned my neck to try to see the screen behind him.

Don't give me lip he said.

But I could already see the red-wine stains on his drooping mouth and neither of us took him seriously.

You go and get something he wheedled and he swayed slightly on the spot.

Through the window I saw a butcherbird swoop it must've spied something on the grass a lizard or an insect maybe a small bird they impale them you know. Stevie told me male butcherbirds impale their prey on forked tree branches then they butcher them using their beaks. Jeez even the birds manage to feed their own chicks around here.

Go on said Sid again pathetically.

Without replying I slid my hand under a cushion and found the remote control I held my finger on the volume button we might've been the only family on the street with a hot TV but we were almost the only one with a remote.

The TV roared then and Sid just about jumped out of his skin.

[illegible] me dead Red he yelped in surprise.

Then he shouted: Soap on a rope go and pick up something for dinner!

Sid had gotten scrawny in the past few weeks I glared at his sunken cheeks his sad doggy jowls even when he went and asserted himself he looked like something you found at the pound.

I rolled my eyes and made a real show of stretching my legs then I stood up.

And turn that thing down he said but I left the remote untouched underneath the couch cushion.

I'll get fish and chips I announced as I walked towards the doorway.

Righto.

But I'm not getting battered the batter gives you heartburn.

Righto.

And I'm getting chicken salt on the chips.

Okay he said and he slunk back to the kitchen without another word he was as useless as tits on a bull.

—

Walking home from the fish-and-chips shop that evening the sky was pink-peach-purple as a bruise yeah it was the whole corporeal spectrum right down to blood red what do they say red sky in the morning sailor's warning red sky at night sailor's in shite. Something like that. I can't remember it wasn't one of Sid's favourites not one of the ones he drummed into my brain. There'd been a couple of old blokes fishing when I walked past on the way to the shop plus a dog all swagger and scars and nosing around the stormwater drain. But they'd given up now the fishermen and the dog and the wharf was deserted and the road was empty even the tide was on its way out.

Small waves pulsed on the sand.

Across the bay the hills rose like a ribcage the last rays of sun cast long shadows I was just rounding the corner yeah there at the point closest to the bay when a car came up behind me it crawled along not wanting to overtake me and even without turning around I knew that it was the cops.

In hindsight I should of made Sid go to the shop who was the parent and who was the kid. But then that would of made things a hundred times worse yeah better for me to deal with the pigs.

I kept walking I was conscious of being watched and of walking like I was conscious of being watched but I wasn't going to be the one to change my pace I refused to turn around and acknowledge that car and it refused to pull ahead of me. We stayed like that the whole way round the bay I didn't speed up my footsteps I didn't swap my fish and chips to my other hand even though the heat through the paper was becoming unbearable I just kept walking and that car never went above ten clicks the two of us were daring the other one to blink trust me I wasn't going to f[illegible] flinch.

It was when we got to the shady area on the far side of the bay yeah there by that shadowy stretch of she-oaks and picnic tables near the concrete mouth of the stormwater drain where that dog had been sniffing around earlier it was there that someone called out my name and I planted my hand on my hip and shoved my hair out of my face and only when I was good and ready did I turn around and see I was being followed by Sergeant Healy.

His patrol car was close enough that I could see him clearly through his open window he was in his uniform for once. I could make out the dark-blue shoulder badge where there were three blue-and-white striped arrowheads yeah three vees. That must've been his rank one two three yeah that was Sergeant Healy the good the bad and the downright ugly see no evil hear no evil speak none neither.

On his sleeve was his patch badge with all the usual crap a crown a laurel wreath a Latin motto nobody could translate. But there in the centre in the middle of his badge captured in mid-flight was a wedge-tailed eagle that monster bird of prey its wings high its neck extended and trapped in its talons was a ruby-red scroll. That scroll read: *Nemesis*.

You want to watch out he said. Girls walking home on their own need to be careful they don't run into trouble.

And I said: Shouldn't it be you who wants to watch out people'll be suspicious of a weirdo that follows girls walking home on their own.

And Sergeant Healy laughed and said I was a ██████ firecracker.

And I knew I should've seen that red sky as a warning or whatever the sailors reckoned.

Where are you going he asked me.

Where does it look like I said.

I was less than two hundred metres from home and heading in that direction.

And Sergeant Healy told me I had a smart mouth. A smart mouth but a good mouth and then he suggested what I might like to do with it and so I suggested Sergeant Healy might like to ██████████ and didn't he hate hearing that from me.

I give the orders around here he said. I give the orders you got that.

And you couldn't really argue not when you were a girl and when you were by the roadside in the half-light-half-shadows because the sun had slunk below the trees and so I never moved but then again neither did he and we stayed like that in a standoff there by the picnic tables and the she-oaks and the yachts sat silent and white in the bay.

You'd better be getting home he said eventually but only after he'd let me sweat and his car skidded in the dirt when he drove off sending up dust and loose gravel his elbow poking proprietarily out the window.

And when I got home I saw that I was shaking. I hate that I let him do that to me.

—

Honest to God I had no idea it was such a big deal when I blew a hole in the police trailer like that. But then I guess some days the scales are tipped in your favour yeah some days the sun's shining on you.

Things started out plainly enough as they always do Stevie and I were doing a little late-night shopping at the petrol station convenience shop. Stevie had a job by now it was nothing special just an after-school number at the supermarket but the pay was better than it was at Madigan's Bookshop on Mann

Street where Stevie used to unpack boxes of new releases for the honour and the glory yeah it's not like his mum ever paid him. But now Stevie was flush yeah he was flash as a rat with a gold tooth and so it fell to me as his closest friend to take him to the servo to spend it.

CC's I said and I pointed to the packet on the shelves. *You can't say no.*

Just say CC's Stevie quoted back obligingly.

He took the chips from the shelf and tucked them under his arm then he turned towards the front of the shop.

Maybe get two bags I said and so Stevie picked up a second bag and slid it in alongside the first.

The servo was empty at that time of night it must've been after ten or so probably late enough for Mrs Madigan to be losing sleep about what Stevie and I might be up to (whereas Sid was hardly going to phone the police). Muzak played over the tinny loudspeaker and I vogued down the aisle towards the cash register bumping rolls of paper towels and packets of instant noodles and boxes of ageing Jatz crackers onto the floor and Stevie shuffled along behind me all pink with embarrassment and clutching his two bags of CC's and scooping groceries up off the floor.

At the counter a service-station attendant barely older than us sat reading something tucked under the bench he didn't look up when I said hello.

There were blue packs of sparklers in a stack on the counter next to fifty-cent bags of mixed lollies and I held up the lollies with one hand and the sparklers with the other and when I turned to Stevie I was grinning.

Good choice. That's what I thought too I said before Stevie could open his mouth.

I chucked the bag of lollies back into their cardboard tray and I placed the sparklers by the cash register there were twenty-four sparklers in each pack.

Guess we'll need some matches too I said to the service-station attendant and pointed to the boxes of Redheads on a shelf behind him.

Because I need more redheads in my life Stevie said.

Just ignore him I told the service-station attendant it's past his bedtime.

Stevie finished paying he was just putting his velcro wallet back in his pocket when I saw the soda bulbs they were on the shelf immediately below the matches there alongside a row of Benson & Hedges cigarettes plus pink Daisy disposable razors those soda bulbs were marked QuickWhip Cream Charges x24. And I could picture them with their foil-sealed ends like little silver birds' eggs yeah they were ready to hatch.

You better give us a box of soda bulbs too. We've run out I explained.

—

We paid again and walked back to my bike we'd left it lying in the car park I could smell salt blowing in off the bay.

Who puts soda bulbs next to matches I said to Stevie that's just asking for trouble.

But Stevie didn't know what I was talking about honestly the life skills I've had to teach that boy and so I told him how to take eight soda bulbs each one containing nitrous oxide and instead of sticking them in your whipped cream dispenser you add some sparkler dust and a little bada bing bada boom and Bob's your uncle and here watch me do it and then you light it and then you underarm it the hell away.

And then what Stevie said.

And then it explodes.

But why Stevie said.

For fun Stevie Wonder for kicks.

Oh then Stevie remembered that actually he'd done this before with his brothers one time don't you know.

Stevie watched me while I worked squatted on my haunches in the empty car park behind the service station.

Got any tape I asked Stevie but he had nothing just two bags of CC's well one and a half he'd started eating without me.

Give me your shoelaces then I said.

And Stevie unthreaded his sneakers obligingly and handed me his laces I wound one around and around and it seemed to hold alright I pulled the ends tight with my teeth. When it was done I passed it to Stevie who turned it over in his hand inspecting my handiwork the knot was neat the sparklers packed tight the whole thing barely bigger than his fist.

We've only got enough shoelaces to make two I said.

Where'd you learn all this he wanted to know.

I wiped sparkler dust from my palms and stood and helped him finish off the first bag of corn chips.

From the school of life Stevie Wonder.

What from Sid?

But that was a laugh because Sid wouldn't know what a soda bulb was if it blew up in his face.

Well what are you gunna do with them? Stevie asked.

We I corrected. What are *we* gunna do with them we're gunna start a revolution Steven.

What tonight? His voice jumped an octave.

—

Sid was always saying I wore my heart on my sleeve and my brains in my boots which was a bit rich coming from him but I guess that night with Stevie was one of those times when I kept my brains down in my socks.

I climbed onto my bike Stevie settled himself wordlessly into the vee of my front handlebars he had the remaining CC's tucked under one arm and the soda bulbs sitting up smartly in his polo-shirt pocket like he was carrying a protractor or something the box of matches nestled neatly beside them.

Hope we don't have a stack and set off your top pocket prematurely I said.

And in the dark it was hard to tell but I could've sworn he was gritting his teeth.

I pushed off from the gutter and we wobbled once twice then we got our balance we cruised round past the front of the petrol station the door was still open and the lights were still blazing but the only sign of life were the bogong moths that butted against the blue security light above the door.

It was hot even at that time of night and the world smelled of salt and gum blossoms I zigzagged us along the empty streets past the shops past the hairdresser with Grace Kelly smouldering in the window past the post office and the TAB past the bait shop.

The moon mooched behind us like a dog.

Where're we headed Stevie said over his shoulder.

The oval? I suggested because I might've been prepared to explode some soda bulbs but I wasn't about to start a bushfire.

We rounded the bend and headed out along the main road then coasted down the hill towards the tennis courts and the oval the sailing club sat sullen in the distance.

What's that Stevie asked as we skidded to a stop in the gravel by the oval.

What's what I said.

Along the far edge of the oval pine trees looked like pencil sketches and through the trees and across the channel were the dark masses of Pelican Island Rileys Island St Huberts Island and beyond that Booker Bay but Stevie was pointing to the trailers parked in the middle of the oval. There was a clump of them sprung up like mushrooms in the grass they were the start of what – a community fair or a market or something. There must have been half-a-dozen trailers and minivans parked all haphazard except for the biggest one a long white one which was parked parallel to the road. That trailer was roughly the size of a small bus it had eight wheels just on the side facing us plus a blunt nose where the truck that towed it into place must've been attached and in the floodlights that turned the world green you could make out the letters on the side of the trailer it read: *New South Wales Police Service Wyoming Local Area Command* make no mistake this was Sergeant Healy's van.

Stevie panicked.

You know once I saw a kid graffiti the skip bins behind the shops he said yeah I was there when he did it and the cops came and took him away they put him in handcuffs and everything he went to juvenile justice for that you know just for some graffiti even though it was his first offence and I don't think you should do this I fully don't and why'd you even bring me down here you said the oval you never said there was a police trailer parked here and what I don't see what's so funny …

I didn't *know* there was a police trailer here I said.

Seriously he said.

I swear. Anyway I said. You've got nothing to worry about you couldn't hit that van if you tried.

—

I'm serious what is it with boys and dares show me just one who'll walk away. When Stevie lit the fuse that was poking out of the bundle he didn't stop and wait for the rest of those sparklers to catch and before I could stop him he pitched the thing into the air for an instant it flew spewing sparks but then it sputtered out it hit the trailer lame and bounced off landing in dry buffalo grass.

Good shot Stevie Wonder I heckled.

Go on then he said.

So I lit the fuse on my soda bulbs and I stood watching its powder neck burn.

Geddridofit Stevie urged he was hopping from one foot to another. But then the most dangerous thing Stevie Madigan had ever done was take the foil off a fresh tin of Milo.

No I waited until that fuse had just millimetres to go yeah until it was seconds away from igniting the rest of the pack and only then did I launch it into the air it was a stream of sparks yeah a real Halley's Comet headed for that police van with its black-and-white chequer band promising *With your help a safe community* and oh my meteor blazed. And when it hit the trailer it exploded it made a helluva bang and the burnt-out soda bulbs landed inside the trailer that's right – the thing blew a hole in the side.

Holy hell Red Stevie shouted. You did it!

And Stevie and I whooped and stomped and he slapped me on the back in the distance a light went on somewhere else a dog began to bark.

We legged it back to the bike but it's hard to run without any laces in your shoes and when you're laughing so hard you can't stand up. I swung the bike upright in the gravel and Stevie arranged himself on the handlebars didn't even worry about the packet of CC's we'd left lying in the dirt and not the burnt soda bulbs we'd left lying in the trailer either and I kicked off and we wobbled back up the hill we were Bonnie and Clyde yeah we were fleeing the scene we were Butch Cassidy and the flipping Sundance Kid.

Did you see that Stevie said. Did you see that hole in the side of the van?

And he laughed because right there by the 'y' in *Wyoming Local Area Command* was a blackened hole almost big enough to pass a football through.

Hole-in-the-wall Wyoming I said sagely as I pedalled us back up the hill.

AND THEN

No jabirus on Jabiru Avenue not the sort of place that does what it says on the tin. No jabirus but plenty of other birds and some of them water birds and waders and everything like moorhens and godwits and lapwings and spoonbills. Like those dirty-feathered long-legged egrets. They'd scavenge in the mud and the muck and the silt down there at the bottom of the hill down where the asphalt peters out and the road swings swiftly to the left and you're only one mistimed clutch change from ending up in the bay.

Down there where the ground is so rotten it would bog a duck.

No jabirus here but plenty of people crammed inside the rickety kitchens of the weatherboard shacks and the post-war redbrick numbers inside the timber-framed fisherman's cottages clad in asbestos and everyone clinging to some kind of hope like they clung to the side of that hill yeah see them there just hanging on.

—

Some days on Jabiru Avenue it was uphill both ways.

—

The Baptists hung a banner from the Gosford overpass that said *Jesus Saves!* It lasted a day before someone graffitied underneath: *Careful they'll take his pension away.*

—

I swear on my mum's grave I didn't know about the sarge's big day when those soda bulbs jumped out of my hand. At least I didn't until Sergeant Healy showed up on our doorstep the very next morning Brylcreem shining in his slick hair.

The hell do you want I said when I opened the door.

Two cops in uniform stood to attention behind him the two of them practically shoulder to shoulder standing there on our pink porch.

Sid can't talk now he's about to head off for work can't afford to be late I said.

But Sergeant Healy wasn't there to see Sid. Said he had smaller fish to fry.

Smaller than Sid I said and I laughed in his face. What – you fishing for minnows these days?

Minors Sergeant Healy corrected me. We're fishing for minors today.

—

Sergeant Healy and his men followed me inside and down the dark corridor and through the lounge room where the blinds were closed and the air was tired and Sid's boxes of junk sagged sadly. We walked that shagpile circuit stepping around coiled cords and brushing past boxes and when we went through the doorway and into the dining room Sid looked up from where he was eating his breakfast and studying the form guide and he just about choked on his Cornflakes.

Morning Sidney boomed Sergeant Healy.

Sergeant said Sid.

And Sid nodded at the officers and he took a stiff swig of his tea. What can I do you for he said.

Not at work yet Sidney said Sergeant Healy. You know what they say about early birds and worms.

He mimed jerking himself off in the middle of our dining room.

That all you came for I said with disgust.

I don't come lightly he said.

He stood there looking slick yeah looking real slippery in his black slacks and his white collared shirt no grubby uniform for our sergeant that day no pale blue like the rest of his plebs.

You were seen Sergeant Healy said to me. *At the scene of the crime.*

Dunno what you're talking about I said.

—

On the table a dozen wrought-iron fence spikes sat in a small plastic tub that said *Sets of six for fifty bucks*. At that price you could bet they were plastic and not the real deal there was no cast iron in there. Still Sergeant Healy prodded the tub like he found it interesting like he was in the market for some fake fleur-de-lis.

No? he said eventually. You don't know anything about a Wyoming Police trailer parked down at the oval ready for Friday's fanfare? Ready to receive the commissioner and the mayor and half the New South Wales Police Service Marching f■king Band. No not ringing any bells?

I looked at him blankly.

What I said. I have seriously no idea what you're talking about.

He'd kept his hand on the tub of fence decorations the whole time he spoke his eyes were their usual icy blue. Now he picked up the tub and he turned to the closest police officer and he clobbered him in the face.

Jesus H. Christ! the constable swore and doubled over he clutched his cheekbone the sharp edge of the plastic tube had split the skin high near his eye and blood rushed to the surface the cut wasn't wide but it looked deep enough who knows it might even need stitches.

What the hell'd you do that for! the officer said holding his forearm to his cheek.

I didn't said Healy.

Honestly you've never seen such a bald-faced lie.

You know what I don't like Healy said turning back to me. I don't like being made to look like a fool not in front of anyone including the commissioner.

Wasn't me I said.

It wasn't you that used soda bulbs to blow a hole in my trailer? he said.

Wasn't anywhere near it I replied. I was at home here with Sid all night.

The cop that was bleeding lowered his forearm from his face and turned to the officer beside him.

Is it okay he said. What does it – does it look like I'm okay?

Get him a tea towel or something Sergeant Healy barked at the second officer who wandered into the kitchen and came back with a stained dishcloth.

Jesus do you want him to get rabies get a clean one said Sergeant Healy.

And so the cop went back into the kitchen and came back again this time he held out an ancient tea towel with faded sunflowers printed on it – it was almost more holes than tea towel.

That'll do Sergeant Healy said and the injured cop held the towel gingerly to his face. He glared at his sergeant over the top of those sunflowers but his sergeant chose not to notice.

I've got an eyewitness says she saw a girl leave the scene – tall – about fifteen years old – with feral red hair and everything Sergeant Healy said. Know anyone who fits that description.

Wasn't me I said again.

But even as I spoke I thought about that service-station attendant who could identify us. About the light that went on immediately after the explosion. And about the dog barking nearby maybe being walked by someone. About all those houses we rode past and all the hundreds of busybodies that could've heard the noise of the explosion and thought they might just phone the cops. But Jesus how was I supposed to know his trailer was for some big thing yeah how could I've known about the commissioner?

Turns out Sergeant Healy didn't care if it was me or not just like it didn't matter if he really had a witness.

I don't give a rat's a█se either way he said. I'm here to arrest you regardless.

—

There were fake fleur-de-lis fence spikes all over the lino where that tub had split when it fell to the floor and they lay like little plastic hieroglyphics and the bleeding constable toed one with his shoe.

That's not fair you can't arrest me – I started to say.

And over at the dining-room table Sid finally found his voice.

Like hell you're going to arrest her he said. Walking in here and talking about arresting people without a reason without a warrant yeah without any skerrick of evidence like hell you're going to arrest Ruby here I'm not gunna let you do that you mongrel.

They were just about the first words Sid had uttered since Sergeant Healy had walked through the door and when he'd finished speaking Sid picked up his form guide and folded it in half and he tucked it under his arm as if the matter was settled but nothing was settled in Healy's mind no he was just getting started.

He spoke slowly and softly and his voice was the sound of an expensive door closing you know the smooth click 'n' lock.

I think it *was* you who blew a hole in my trailer Sergeant Healy said to me. I think it was you – you and your little mate Steven Madigan – and I think you did it to try to embarrass me in front of the commissioner and I think you're going to pay for it now.

You can't arrest me I scoffed though deep down I wasn't sure no I wasn't so hot on the legalities back then but wasn't that the wrong thing to say to Sergeant Trevor James Healy of Wyoming Police Force he didn't like advice from a girl.

Can't I! Can't I! he said. Ruby McCoy I'm arresting you at eight-oh-seven-ay-em on Wednesday the twenty-third for assaulting Police Officer Stanley here.

He indicated to the officer holding our sunflower tea towel to his face.

You did that!

I was incensed.

Let's get you down to the station said Healy.

As if I said.

And now we can charge you with resisting arrest he said.

What – but I haven't even —

And also with indecent and offensive language —

I never swore —

And that's what we call the trifecta he said.

But I haven't done any of those things I said hotly.

You're resisting arrest he said.

Get f█ed.

That's two out of three he crowed.

And I swore at him again because I never did know when to pull my head in no I never knew when I was beat.

Ah we'll get this into a children's court he said and he almost sounded sad that the whole thing had been so easy.

We'll get it through too he said on the evidence provided by my witnesses here.

And he gripped Constable Stanley firmly by the shoulder jolting his hand away from the cut on his face.

You can't arrest her Sid said. She hasn't done anything wrong and anyway she's only a kid.

But they handcuffed me the metal was heavy and cold against my skin it was cold against the summery day and outside somewhere a lawnmower moaned and in the distance the *clang-clang-clang* of a school bell.

You people don't know how to help yourselves Healy said to Sid and he laughed like he found us funny then he let the smile fall from his face. He ushered me to the doorway that led to the kitchen then he paused and turned back to Sid.

Unless … Healy said to him.

Unless what Sid said.

Unless you might be willing to do a trade.

Sergeant Healy let the words hang while the blood drained from Sid's face and whatever nerve Sid showed moments ago was now puddling down there in his thongs.

A trade he said weakly.

You heard me said Sergeant Healy.

He left me standing handcuffed in the doorway to the kitchen while he walked to the dining-room table where he produced a grey hundred-dollar note from his pocket and it was worn with age and creased and soft and he smoothed the paper between his fingers and he placed it on the table.

See that – said Sergeant Healy.

Sid eyed that grey nurse.

They always say you can pick an undercover cop because they use fresh notes Sergeant Healy said. Nothing too crisp about that one is there Sidney.

That's the genuine article Sergeant Healy said. That's come from a drug bust just imagine if I loaded you up with that thing Sidney just think about that for a moment. Are you imagining that Sidney I could take the handcuffs off your kid and I could put them on you instead I could take you down to the station right now Sidney you could stop her from being charged just like that.

He clicked his fingers.

Are you following all this Sidney. Are you catching my drift are you are you because I can't hear you taking up my kind offer don't tell me you're all piss and vinegar Sidney what you'd sell your kid down the river —

He doesn't have to say anything! I said talking over the top of the sergeant and taking the decision out of Sid's hands. My dad doesn't have to do any trade because I'm not gunna let him okay.

I twisted my wrists awkwardly inside their cuffs they'd been cold when Sergeant Healy put them on me but now I discovered the metal was wet with sweat.

Ruby said Sid. Ruby I … Rube —

He looked more hangdog than ever.

Red he said finally.

Yeah?

I'll come and pick you up from the station he said.

And I knew what Sid was thinking even without his saying I could see his plan as plain as day. Yeah Sid knew the cops would go easy on me because I was only a kid at the same time he knew Healy was gunning for him oh they'd throw the book at Sid given half a chance. Make no mistake Sergeant Healy had come there with the sole aim of stitching up my dad but we'd beaten that dog Healy at his own game by refusing to trade places yeah we won oh don't you muck with Sid and me yeah we're the real thing we are the real McCoy.

And when I was escorted across the front lawn to the cop car that morning and the sun blazed bright overhead I tilted my face to the clear sky and I drank in the morning smells. Cut grass and victory. Across the road at number six Mr Anders was still watering his dahlias like nothing had changed and I nodded and raised my cuffed wrists in acknowledgement but I must've transformed fully into Medusa by then because Mr Anders he wouldn't meet my eyes.

—

The highway patrol car that day was a 1978 Ford Falcon XC 500 what you think Sid taught me nothing it was one of them coke-bottle Falcons with a near-four-litre engine and a three-speed auto and a *tap-tap-tappet* as the engine got going but even it had enough sense to shut up once the hydraulic lifters cleared.

Sergeant Healy sat in the front passenger seat with his knees brushing the glove box and his comb-over touching the roof while the not-bleeding cop got to drive. Between them on the centre console was a grey two-way radio and a black walkie-talkie and a bunch of other junk besides then high on the dash sat a large box that read *miles per hour* and *speed minder* and *solid state radar* and a bright-orange button screaming *violate*.

Constable Stanley sat in the back seat with me he was still holding our tea towel to his head. I ignored him and sank down in my bucket seat and stared out the window and the yellow vinyl of the seat stuck to the backs of my legs the stitching printing bars on my thighs.

We headed uphill and away from the bay and through the boxy back window I watched Jabiru Avenue retreat. It rolled by slowly at first Mr Anders's place and the Allsopps' joint and then the Langerfords' further up the hill all those peeling picket fences all those scrap-metal patchwork carports they recoiled from the cop car and receded into the distance yeah Jabiru Avenue was bowing out.

—

They took me to Wyoming Police Station past Yattalunga Police Station and Gosford Police Station oh Sergeant Healy he wasn't bound by jurisdiction like the great unwashed. There I sat in an airless broom cupboard out the back if this were the interview room just imagine the cells.

Name?

I reckon you could hazard a guess I said.

State your name for the record said Constable Stanley and he pointed to the tape recorder on the table between us.

I noticed he'd abandoned that tea towel from our kitchen and his cheek was swollen yeah shiny and red but that gash was pretty miniscule where the edge of the tub had split the skin honestly I don't know what he'd been carrying on about.

Ruby Sherrin McCoy I said sourly.

Sharon?

Sherrin.

His eyebrows shot up. Like the football?

Like the name.

Then I leaned closer to the machine that sat between us: But I only answer to Red.

Miss McCoy do you understand why you've been brought in here today.

Because you d■kheads are all corrupt I supplied.

Language said Constable Stanley but you could see his heart wasn't in it.

You are but I said. You and I both know it was your mate Sergeant Healy that did that to your face. Far out he must hold you in real high esteem that the only job he trusts you with around here is target practice is that it.

Between us the light on the tape recorder blazed and in the silence I could hear the tape whirr.

It doesn't have to be this way you know said Constable Stanley after a long pause. You're so young you have your whole life ahead of you —

Actually you'd better check the tape to see what Constable Stanley said because I'd well and truly tuned out. Spare me the sympathy and the pep talk yeah spare me your pity Jesus where's Sid's violin when you need it.

Do you have a lawyer Constable Stanley asked me.

Yeah I just can't remember where I left her I said patting my pockets.

Can I call Legal Aid for you.

I give in. Are they as useless as you lot?

You don't seem very worried for someone who's sitting in a police station. And he almost sounded impressed.

Way I see it today was a victory I said. You wanted Sid and you only got me think I'll chalk that one up to the McCoys.

He stopped the tape then and we sat in silence and we watched the red light fade away. Constable Stanley removed the cassette from inside and he held it up to the light and he wound the tape backwards with a pen then he turned the tape front to back like he suspected it might be faulty and he put it into his top pocket and he replaced his pen beside it.

You're not actually under arrest he said you've been brought in voluntarily to assist us with our enquiries.

Doesn't feel very ████ voluntary.

Did you hear what I said you're not under arrest I'm not charging you with anything here.

So what I'm free to go?

You are.

What like right now I'm free to go right now?

Don't make a song and dance about it he said.

But I don't understand why did Healy say I was being arrested if you're here saying I'm not.

Constable Stanley rubbed the back of his neck he closed his eyes briefly like I made him feel tired.

Because Sergeant Healy made the mistake of thinking that might be enough to scare you he said.

But why ask me if I want a lawyer if you already know you're gunna let me go.

It's called due process some of us actually follow it.

Not many I've met I said.

And he raised his eyebrows sharply this time.

Now I can't very well let you walk out there yet or people will ask questions he said. But if you sit tight for ten minutes and keep your head down then I'll show you off the premises after that.

And if I don't keep my head down then you'll cop another box of fence spikes to the head.

No if you don't keep your head down he said then you'll find Sergeant Healy is conducting this interview instead of me.

—

According to the oversized clock on the wall we were only six minutes into my ten-minute stint in the interview room but apparently my ability to keep my head down only stretched so far.

Reckon it must be tempting I said. All day long you're busting your balls chasing criminals that are out there making ten times what you take home in your pay.

But it must've crossed his mind. What while crims are out there getting rich and he's following his due process and he can barely make the mortgage repayments and his wife's getting thingy about the fact they can't afford to holiday anywhere north of Budgewoi and what he's not tempted to earn a little something on the side I don't think so either.

Reckon it must be real tempting I said.

And Constable Stanley sighed in that way that teachers do when you ask if this is going to be in the exam.

Not to me he said.

He was fiddling with the empty tape recorder on the table while he spoke opening and closing and reopening that little perspex cassette door until I wanted to move it out of his reach.

What you're not tempted I said. Or you are but you don't go through with it?

Neither he said. I'm not tempted and I don't do it.

They all do but I said. I thumbed towards the rest of the building.

But Constable Stanley sat impassive he refused to say anything.

Mostly it's to do with cutting corners he said eventually. You know doing what's required to get a conviction across the line even if that means ignoring a few rules you'd be surprised how the system is set up against you how hard it is to put the right people away.

Stop wasting your time on the wrong ones then I said.

He smiled wryly and he stood up from the table touching that egg on his head gingerly.

Why does Healy hate you I said.

Because I'm a university-educated pussy he quoted. Better question: why does he hate *you*.

I stood up and I was the same height as Constable Stanley.

Uh reckon it's got something to do with my name I said thinking about all those McCoys the Healys had hated I was the last in a long line it seemed.

What Sherrin? asked Constable Stanley.

And I actually laughed at that.

—

Outside Wyoming Police Station the day was dazzling yeah it were blindingly bright like stepping out of the movies after the pensioner session I was still seeing stars when I spotted Sid he was parked across the road and up a bit.

He was in his blue Stubbies and matching blue thongs. His Mount Panorama t-shirt must've been in the wash oh but he was wearing a t-shirt and not his work shirt I noted yeah he'd taken the morning off for me.

Behind him was a line-up of Norfolk Island pines those trees were dark and cool and standing there Sid had the decency to look pint-sized for once it took a forty-metre tree to dwarf him.

He stood leaning against the car it was the Sunbird today had been the Sunbird for a while now yeah ever since he got busy working for Sergeant Healy Sid'd had less time to dabble in used cars. That Holden Sunbird took roost in the carport at home you couldn't miss it – thing was Tweety-bird yellow. Seriously when was he gunna get over that Datsun he kept seeking out shades of (fool's) gold.

That Sunbird was a two-door hatchback but then two doors was all we'd ever need he waved when he saw me his grin splitting his face.

Ruby Tuesday he announced to the street.

He could hardly keep his long limbs still.

—

Did they treat you alright Sid asked. They didn't hurt you did they did they did that bloke lay a finger on you if he did I'll turn the car around right now oh I'll be back there like a shot.

(Only he waited until we were on the freeway and travelling in the wrong direction before he started making those sorts of threats.)

It wasn't him that interviewed me I told Sid. It was Constable Stanley.

What the one that copped the you know – Sid pointed to the side of his face.

That's him I said.

Well what did he say.

Dunno it was weird he just let me go.

What with no warning or nothing?

Yeah I said. He kept me talking for a bit and then he let me off the hook.

Clear conscience clear record! Sid said.

—

We never spoke about the fact that Sid didn't switch places when Healy gave him the chance some things don't need discussing. He was doing it for me yeah the whole time for me what kid needs their dad in custody.

—

On the drive home Sid sang all the usual suspects that included 'Hi-Yo Silver' safe to say. His fingers danced across the top of the steering wheel not worrying that the car handled like a dog on a lino floor. Yeah that Sunbird drove like a Torana that's missing its engine the express bus would've got me home faster. On pension day those buses ran every seven minutes.

But then the express bus didn't come with buckskin velour seat covers and it didn't come with a roll of Peppermint Life Savers there on the dash. And the tyres made their happy *frrrp frrrp* noise on the road like a book when you flipped the pages at speed. And out the open window birds sat threaded on telegraph wires small and bright like Sid's fishing lures.

—

Sid responded to our close shave with Sergeant Healy and the law in the only way he knew how: by seeing it as a sign that our luck had changed for the good yeah in Sid's book we'd hit a rich vein. It's a sign he told me confidently. This is the start of a winning streak I could've been sitting in a cell in Wyoming staring at Healy's ugly mug but instead I'm here at home with you.

Out on Jabiru Avenue the sky was so blue it almost took your breath away the heat was as tight as a vice. There was a permanent soundtrack of shrieking and splashing and bombing as the neighbourhood kids flocked to the bay at the bottom of the hill to float on faded li-los and to fish and swim and to fling themselves off the old jetty.

And Sid caught the bug he got that demob-happy feeling you could see it in the way he paraded around the house his blue thongs thwacking his t-shirt flapping while he played his violin. Any idiot could see he was working up a plan yeah he was getting ready to put his head back on the chopping block that's right Sid was plotting his next business venture he was having his next big idea.

—

Dried meat he told me triumphantly one morning. Biltong's the way to go.

Bil-what?

I never even tried to hide my disdain.

Biltong it's a delicacy in South Africa Ruby Red.

Long way from Jabiru Avenue I said.

But Sid reckoned there was an untapped market for dried meat here too who knew who could've seen this one coming. And so every day restaurant quantities of beef strips were cured in salt and doused in vinegar and threaded onto S-hooks made out of galvanised wire and all done on our cracked kitchen bench and after that they were suspended from all four sides of our clothesline where they swung gently in the afternoon breeze.

Scenic I said.

I stood at the back door and watched strips of beef backstrap in various stages of decay dangling on the clothesline.

You charging extra for the salmonella I wanted to know.

Mates' rates for you Sid winked.

Where'd you get it I asked.

What the meat? I know a bloke. Sorted me out with a good price.

Is it road kill.

Don't be cheeky it's prime beef Peter Russell-Clarke would sell his mother for this.

Peter Brussel-Sprout? Sure if he likes botulism.

—

I was dark with Sid not over the biltong no not that – I couldn't care less how he salted his steak. I was angry he refused to see our luck had run out that we'd used it all up on Sergeant Healy specifically in preventing Sid getting arrested.

It's Nemesis and the scales of justice I said to him. You're forgetting how it works you know the winged balancer of life. I held up *The Golden Treasury of Greek Mythology* with its soft green cover. The scales of justice I reminded him sharply. You know the light and the dark the good and the bad for every good thing an equally bad thing is coming and you've used up all our luck lately.

Fairy stories Sid said. When good luck comes visiting you offer it a beer and a place to sit down haven't I taught you anything Ruby Tuesday.

And he laughed and shook his head ruefully.

—

At the bottom of the hill by the belly of the bay was an upturned dinghy it wasn't our boat it wasn't anybody's but Stevie and I we'd claimed it as our own.

That dinghy was a timber clinker grown ancient with flaking blue paint barely six foot at best that thing had sat there so long its cleats were covered in rust its gunwales sunk into the sand.

The Good Ship Progress we named it because that boat was going nowhere. Even if it wanted to it was marooned high above the tide line and hemmed in by mangroves its sides half submerged in the silt. Still we'd go there at night and I'd sit at the stern with Stevie as first mate and we'd sail to nowhere on that abandoned dinghy that sat bum up to the stars.

You being bitten? asked Stevie and he scratched his arms.

Nah mosquitos don't like me as much as you I said. That's why I bring you along.

On the shoreline the she-oaks shushed in the dark bowing and tossing their heads but above us the night sky was bright it was all silver-scaled and clear.

That's Sirius I said pointing.

Are you Sirius.

Deadly I said.

Yahoo Sirius?

Seeing Sirius is a bad omen I said.

Stevie squinted. A bad omen for every person in the southern hemisphere? Half the planet can probably see Sirius tonight he said.

I shrugged in the dark.

When Achilles was approaching Troy he saw Sirius in the sky and it was an evil omen I said.

My mum really opened a can of worms when she gave you that book didn't she.

Sirius is the Dog Star too I offered.

And Stevie approved of that. That's the saucepan just above it he said maybe the Dog Star's looking for a feed.

He should come to our place in that case Sid's got rotting beef strips strung up all over the place. And I told Stevie about the new biltong business about how Sid was set to make his fortune.

He thinks he's on a lucky streak because he didn't get arrested I said.

Hmm doesn't sound all that lucky to me Stevie said.

But then Stevie hadn't had Sergeant Healy on the doorstep after we'd both chucked those soda bulbs. Yeah it's one rule for us and no rules for the rest yeah you tell me we're not victimised.

Out on the bay a putt putt drifted along its lantern slow-blinking its motor *pop-popping* regular as a heartbeat.

Did you know I'm going to buy a boat soon said Stevie he must have been listening to that putt putt too.

Not one like this he said he patted the hull of the clinker. But a real boat a cruiser.

That right? I said.

Yeah maybe after Christmas I'll buy it.

You expecting a windfall.

Don't need one Stevie said. I've already got my grandpa's war medals they're worth heaps don't you know.

You'd *sell* your grandpa's war medals.

But Stevie wasn't listening.

A cruiser you know a proper cabin cruiser twin-engine outboard motor 23- no a 26-footer … You could buy one too he added.

What with your pop's medals.

No with yours he said.

Pep didn't serve in the war.

Who Stevie said.

Pep my pop he didn't serve in the war.

What do you call him that for?

What Pep. You've heard me call him that before it's short for — well it's not short for anything anymore he died ages ago but the family always used to call him Pep it's a long story and anyway he doesn't have any war medals so I guess I'll have to ride in your cruiser.

Stevie considered this for a bit.

If there's room he conceded. It's only a 26-footer you know.

Out on the bay that putt putt chugged contentedly in the dark.

Did you know my pop was at the bombing of Darwin have I ever told you that Stevie said. He was one of the first ones to sound the alarm yeah he saw the Japanese planes arrive you know when they first flew in across the harbour.

Your mum's dad I asked like that was the important bit.

Yeah Stevie confirmed the one with the Zorro bobble cape. He was swimming in the harbour when he saw the planes —

What Darwin Harbour? Can you even swim in Darwin Harbour there's crocodiles I bet.

He was swimming in the harbour Stevie repeated. He was really into swimming he swam every day of his life.

That why you've got his war medals and not your older brothers? I said. Because you're such a good swimmer like him?

And Stevie shoved me off the dinghy and onto the wet sand.

But seriously the stories we all tell ourselves.

—

Those biltong strips stayed strung up around our backyard for days just gently rotting in the sun strange soundless wind chimes like stiff brown tongues yeah those meat strips were calcified sound. They dripped from the trees and they hung from the clothesline they spun slowly in the afternoon sea breeze then when the southerly picked up those strips flapped horizontal as wings like birds trying to take off from a wire.

Except when the kookaburras and the butcherbirds got to them yeah then those strips really took flight.

—

They called Pep a traitor when he deserted the army called him a dog and then they beat him and they set fire to his dresses and they just about burned up Pep too. He was hospitalised with second-degree burns to both of his arms from his fingertips to his biceps. They had to do it they said to teach him a lesson yeah to teach him he'd hung his army mates out to dry.

Afterwards they told him not to report what happened not to the cops not to nobody. Said they'd cut out his tongue if he ever said a word they'd cut it out and hang it from a tree.

—

It was too late to hope Sid and Chook might escape a call-up from Sergeant Healy that vessel had already sailed.

Sid and Chook's jobs at the power station had dried up by then and so when Sid wasn't boiling biltong or salting biltong or ferrying laundry-basket loads of biltong back and forth to the backyard where he'd drape dripping strips of meat from the washing-line wires like little bloodied flags of war yeah in between all of that Sid was now running regular errands for the sergeant yeah Sid and Chook were Healy's stooges.

What kinda things does he get you to do I wanted to know but Sid didn't give much away.

This and that he said.

What sort of this and that what stuff specifically.

Courier stuff specifically he said.

But that didn't explain why his hands shook uncontrollably whenever he got home shook so much he wasn't fit to lift his violin. Wasn't fit to cook his own dinner even but then that was no real change there.

—

One of the things Sid did tell me about was the truck stop at Berowra but that's only because he went there so often it was his home away from Jabiru Avenue. The Berowra truck-checking station was on the side of the road yeah there near the tollbooths on the Pacific Highway. There were sheer cliffs on either side of the highway great whacking walls of sandstone.

Stevie told me that Robert Redford scouted out the area for a spaghetti western once but I can't imagine Robert Redford getting excited about the F1 truck stop.

That highway was the main transport artery heading north out of Sydney so those tollbooths were hardly inconspicuous there in full view of the commuters and the holidaymakers and the flatbeds and the tanker trucks and the articulated semitrailers that were ferrying blue metal crushed stone sand gravel timber and steel tonnes of it to and from Sydney every day.

But Sid said Sergeant Healy liked the truck stop as a drop-off point precisely because the highway was busy yeah nothing like hiding something in plain sight he told Sid and Chook nothing like shoving it right up their nostrils.

As for Sid and Chook they liked the fact that it was only thirty minutes up the road twenty-five if Chook was driving and he usually did that meant they could do the sergeant's dirty work and be back at the White Hart in just over an hour barely time for their bar stools to miss their bums.

Yeah Sid and Chook got it down to a fine art alright they had it down pat. They got real familiar with that road to Berowra and when they arrived at the truck-weighing station they knew the routine too. Pair of them were smooth as a couple of dancers. Sometimes they were picking up and sometimes they were dropping off but always the packages looked plain enough. Unmarked envelopes of cash or unmarked envelopes of white powder occasionally an old blue travel bag with *Ansett Airways* printed along the side. And that cracked vinyl bag with its cream-coloured piping was just as unremarkable as all those plain envelopes only it was a helluva lot heavier.

Yeah they knew the drill alright knew to stay in the car seatbelts fastened no sudden movements no names no eye contact no smart talk no talk at all if you liked your fingers where they were now what brings you fellas here looking for directions are youse tourists nice day for it don't you reckon real nice day. Then bills counted goods eyeballed pleasure doing business with you boys you enjoy your day out together now won't you. And drive off real steady yeah drive away slow and don't go checking the rear-view mirror and windows down radio up like none of it ever happened yeah as if you hadn't been fraternising with the friend of your enemy like you hadn't done a job for the cops. But a beer could help with that and six beers even better Sid and Chook drank their shame clean away.

—

Then one day Sid and Chook showed up at the truck stop primed to do a delivery like always the blue travel bag sagged on the back seat of Chook's Sandman nothing unusual there. While in the front Sid and Chook would've been bickering about boozing or batting averages or bloody biltong recipes the radio rusted onto their country music station Sid's fingers dancing unstoppably along the windowsill.

We had no idea Sid said morosely in the courtroom afterwards.

He wasn't wrong what a pair of mugs him and Chook they didn't have a clue.

No neither of them saw anything strange about the fact that the truck stop was deserted in the middle of a Friday morning when it was usually chock-a-block full of truckies at that day and time. There were no six-cylinder engines no crunch of gravel no monotony of tyres just a hot wind swirling around the compound flicking dust and sand against the duco plus the rattle of skeleton weeds.

Just like they didn't think anything of it when that emptiness was broken by a white van that pulled up to collect the tollbooth takings at the exact same moment Chook's Sandman arrived it happened like f████ clockwork.

No they didn't blink when three security guards got out of that soft-skin vehicle what the security company didn't feel like sending them out in an armoured car that day they said no go in a panel van why don't you. Meanwhile the security guards themselves wore clean khaki uniforms but no bulletproof vests yeah they looked like they'd never done a day's security work in their lives oh they kept their uniforms squeaky clean and they left their protective vests at home what's more they kept their gun holsters bare yeah they were suspiciously empty.

Hell the only thing to suggest they were security guards sent to empty the tollbooth takings was their cash bag which one of the guards carried in his hand and was helpfully labelled *CASH* in great big f█k-off letters.

And when those security guards opened the rear doors of their van they exposed their cargo to the savage summer sun and then they just left the twin doors gaping. They walked over to Sid and Chook who were parked there in the dust they spoke through Chook's wound-down driver's window.

Got something we can take off your hands fellas said the security guard.

Do I look like a tollbooth that needs emptying replied Chook.

What you look like is a couple of homosexuals said the guard but I'm not after that sort of delivery.

—

Beside the Sandman the security guard rubbed the stubble on his chin slowly like he was tossing up between the steak and the veal.

You're Healy's blokes right he said.

You'd better step out of the car and show us what you've got he added.

Doesn't work like that sunshine said Sid.

The security guard straightened up then he stepped back from Chook's window almost treading on his two mates standing behind him and he laced his fingers at the base of his skull.

What. You're not gunna hand over the goods he said. I took you two for dills but I didn't think you were that stupid you know Healy'll feed you to the sharks.

And Sid said that's not how it works they weren't getting out to give him a demonstration it wasn't a flipping Tupperware party. But the security guard said he wasn't taking any goods that he hadn't viewed properly.

We try before we buy around here he said.

Youse can help yourselves then said Chook and he nodded towards the blue *Ansett Airways* travel bag on the back seat. And what are you doing picking up this stuff anyway whoever heard of security guards receiving for the pigs.

Whoever heard of dropkicks like you two working for someone like Healy the security guard said. Now get your blue handbag and get out of the car and show us the goods you gutless wonders.

So Sid and Chook got out of the Sandman and they took those shotguns out of the blue travel bag and they held them up dumbly on display.

—

The way Sid remembers it the cops came from nowhere they arrived gliding in on that hot gritty wind dive-bombing in like buzzards.

Yeah vultures that's right [illegible] ornithological undertakers. And Sid and Chook walking corpses what a pair. Sirens wailed and at the same time a bullhorn barked those cop cars sent blue lights crawling up the cliff walls.

—

Yeah the way Sid remembers it the security guards fell into position it was like they'd been instructed what to do. Legs apart and arms up in mock surrender they looked like toy plastic GI Joes. And the guards formed one point of a triangle where Sid and Chook comprised the dazed second angle and the security van with its dusty white doors blowing back and forth in the breeze made up the open-mouthed third.

Drop the weapons and put your hands above your heads

that bullhorn bellowed. Drop the weapons. And. Put. Your. Hands. Above. Your. Heads.

The sound system crackled static in the canyon.

Drop the weapons!

And so Sid and Chook put the shotguns down in the chalky dust the bullet chambers were oiled and empty.

We're not armed Chook yelled you bastards we're not even armed.

—

The cops moved in then running swarming fanning out they were bent low shoulders hunched boots crunching on gravel and the round black muzzles of their Glocks jerked and yanked and their belt buckles flashed in the dazzle.

They went for Chook first. Because he was closer and because of his size you wouldn't pick off Tom before Jerry. He stood near Sid but even at that proximity and even with his arms raised Chook hardly cast shade onto Sid.

The first cop to reach Chook took the butt of his police-issue weapon and he rammed it into Chook's stomach Chook grunted and doubled up and the pig cracked the gun down the back of Chook's head Chook slumped softly into the dirt. A second cop this one taller oh this one could look Sid in the eye if he wasn't so morally bankrupt this pig thumped Sid behind the knees he fell forward in prayer a gun was held up to Sid's pulsing temple.

Such is life eh Sidney he said.

—

Those three security guards went on the record to say that Chook and Sid carried out a cash-in-transit robbery while armed with dangerous weapons it was a staggering lie. Oh *allegedly* Sid and Chook demanded cash while *allegedly* holding the three security guards at gunpoint even more insulting they were *allegedly* amateurs.

—

It was a ruthless brazen opportunistic act of violence Sergeant Healy told the Crown Prosecutor. A case of — He paused for effect. You see the cards you play the cards he said.

You see the cards you play the cards? the judge repeated.

Those were the defendant's own words Your Honour this was a callous attack that was carried out with no planning or forethought the defendants simply saw the cash-in-transit van parked at the Berowra-Calga Tollway toll plaza and noting that the southbound weighbridge and surrounding areas were otherwise deserted they decided to take advantage of the situation. A cold-blooded *carpe diem* if you'll excuse my Latin Your Honour.

Latin is always welcome in my court Sergeant.

As it should be Your Honour.

Next the Crown Prosecutor said it is your belief then Sergeant from what you witnessed at the scene that the defendants were not acting with any level of professionalism in carrying out the alleged robbery and that it was not a premeditated attack.

That is correct.

And is that possible Sergeant? Is it possible to see a cash-in-transit security van parked by the Berowra-Calga Tollway toll plaza when you didn't know it was there and you weren't looking out for it and while travelling in a vehicle along the Pacific Freeway?

It is.

While travelling at speed Sergeant?

With respect this is the Berowra-Calga Tollway toll plaza we're talking about and not Piccadilly Circus. It would have been entirely possible to see the security van there the whole thing the whole one-kilometre stretch of side road was completely barren at the time bar a great whacking security van with *CashCorp Security* plastered along both sides.

You're saying it was possible then.

Yes it was possible he told the prosecution.

And so having seen the security van there the defendants made a split-second decision to attempt an armed robbery this is your assertion Sergeant?

Yes it is.

Sergeant would you tell the court how you came to that conclusion.

Certainly for a start CIT armed robbers wear —

For the benefit of the court Sergeant by CIT you mean—

Cash-in-transit.

Thank you Sergeant.

CIT armed robbers or armed robbers targeting cash-in-transit vehicles wear disguises as a rule Healy said. Balaclavas wigs sunglasses stocking masks offenders generally go to great lengths to protect their identity sixty-nine percent of all CIT armed robbery offenders in this country know enough to cover their faces.

And yet the defendants did not.

The defendants may as well have posed for a photo.

Thank you Sergeant.

There's also the issue of their getaway car.

Sergeant?

The type of vehicle used by CIT offenders tells us a lot about the professionalism of the outfit. We're seeing a trend towards luxury-type cars. One in ten chooses a Mercedes Benz seventeen percent opt for a high-performance sports car Mitsubishi is a popular pick offenders want to be fast and they want to be inconspicuous. The defendants drove a 1974 three-speed Holden Sandman hardly what you'd call a quick getaway.

Thank you Sergeant.

Would've been faster to crawl.

Thank you Sergeant.

Or tie their legs together for a three-legged race.

Sergeant may I remind you that this is a court of law the judge jumped in again.

Yes Your Honour.

Before you leave the stand said the Crown Prosecutor please tell the court how much money the offenders stood to gain from the attempted robbery.

Ah the exact amount is unknown. Although in my experience and studies have shown that the risk-to-yield ratio of unplanned armed robberies means the amounts involved are pretty paltry. We're talking hundreds and rarely thousands. The cash-in-transit company has confirmed the tollbooths were emptied the previous day and any mug can tell you the expressway's only fifty cents one way and so it stands that the defendants were only set to gain small change —

Sergeant.

It was amateur hour.

Sergeant! How much money did the defendants stand to gain from the attempted armed robbery?

We don't know to the dollar.

Sergeant are you telling me you don't know how much money the defendants stood to gain from the attempted armed robbery?

That's correct.

Does this mean the money was never recovered Sergeant?

That's correct.

The money is still missing?

Again correct.

But how is that possible Sergeant the alleged offenders were apprehended at the scene am I to believe you let them keep the proceeds of their crime as a souvenir?

Ah there was a third accomplice —

A third accomplice! Why is the court only being made aware of this now Sergeant the judge cut in again.

A third accomplice Your Honour who fled the scene with the proceeds.

On foot Sergeant?

Like I said this was not a professional outfit Your Honour.

But professional enough Sergeant that a third accomplice was able to flee the scene with the proceeds.

That's my understanding yes Your Honour. You have to remember Your Honour this was a highly volatile and rapidly evolving situation we're talking about the defendants were armed with high-powered weaponry and they were desperate they were unpredictable. The lives of three security guards were at stake three *on-duty* security guards carrying out their jobs these men have families Your Honour they have wives and children to go home to and if they don't go home to those wives and children because they've been shot in the line of duty well then you know who has to knock on the door and deliver that news Your Honour it's my men that's who get that grim task it's my men Your Honour. It was a miracle lives weren't lost that day Your Honour and that's all down to me and my men being so quick to arrive on the scene.

Sergeant the court acknowledges the efforts of the New South Wales Police Service.

Thank you Your Honour I —

If I may stop you there Sergeant.

Your Honour.

Then the Crown Prosecutor said was there a cash-degradation system in place a dye bomb or some other security measure installed by the security company so that it's possible to trace the stolen money to ascertain where it is now?

I'm afraid not.

There was no such system in place Sergeant?

That money is impossible to trace.

But isn't that unorthodox Sergeant surely a reputable cash-in-transit security company such as CashCorp Security would have tracing measures in place?

That's a little out of my jurisdiction I'm afraid you'll have to ask CashCorp about that.

Thank you Sergeant you may leave the stand.

—

You've never seen a court case with so many holes a f■king criminal-jurisdiction colander. For a start that security van was totally unmarked it never said *CashCorp Security* on the side and why would Sid and Chook try to hold up a plain white panel van.

Second there was never any third accomplice who shot through with the proceeds of crime. That's because there were no proceeds and no crime either thanks for asking.

And those shotguns at the heart of Sergeant Healy's sob story? Those guns were never loaded not a single lonely bullet not to mention the fact that they were Healy's own guns. What a pack of lies pack of mongrels that Healy couldn't lie straight in bed.

—

Sid was sentenced to six years imprisonment with four years non-parole for actual daylight robbery. Chook got the same six years with four years non-parole the two of them were going down together. I sat silent at their sentence hearing they'd both pleaded guilty not much point saying otherwise not when it was their word against Sergeant Healy's who's going to listen to them.

And stuck to the door of the court that day was a laminated sign that said: *No muddy or fluorescent work clothes to be worn into this courtroom* as if labourers' fluoros were as offensive as out and out filth. Sid didn't wear fluoro or grime as he shuffled into the sentencing hearing no he and Chook wore their prison greens yeah two peas in a prison-green pod. With their green collarless shirts and their green beltless trousers their regulation socks in their laceless velcro shoes. And Sid wore a matching green seasick expression as the judge read out his sentence.

There was a buzz in my brain all the way through the hearing it was dull and low and constant like maybe they were drilling in some part of the building like someone was drilling in my head. Six years with four years non-parole that courtroom had the same suffocating feel as that backroom in Wyoming Police Station. Both rooms were stale with sealed windows the kind that come standard in government buildings but it was more than that those rooms were gagging like chewing on dry cotton balls and to crack your mouth open a millimetre was to feel your tongue turn to sand. Six years with four years non-parole those bastards stitched Sid and Chook up.

—

Yeah it was entrapment the entire crime was paperback fiction yeah payback where none was owed and where the scales of justice were already on the floor in our favour. Those dogs loaded up Sid and Chook with weapons and then they invented a crime that didn't happen and then they held the line yeah those mongrels stuck to their version of events. But that's not even the most disgusting part no the most disgusting thing the bit that really kills me is how offensively easy the whole thing was. Easy come easy go easy as a ████ Sunday morning so easy the sergeant never even worked up a sweat.

I put a hole smaller than your fist in the side of Healy's caravan and so now Sid was going away for four years and maybe six if he didn't play his cards right. Yeah it was offensive how easy it was for the pigs to put us in our place disgusting how easy it was for them to put us down.

—

So no. The way Sid remembers it is not the way it's been told and it's definitely not the way that it happened. As he walked to the doorway heading down to the cells yeah as he exited the court that day he went with a sheriff at both slumping shoulders plus a third pressed up hard at his back.

And I was waiting for a sign from Sid you know a nod or a wink just to say he had a plan tucked up his short green sleeve. All I got was a stricken glance and there was no scheming in that. But worse: he was too ashamed to meet my eye.

—

I lost my dad and my mum that day in court Sid was both things Sid was all things. Sid was it.

Sid was crabs that scuttled happily back into the bay because he didn't have the heart to hold them in his net. Sid was suicide missions down Jabiru Avenue on a pink two-wheeler bike while he cheered. Sid was a holey 1976 Mount Panorama t-shirt and too-short Stubbies shorts while he played his Mendini in the kitchen. He was bedtime stories straight from the form guide. Sid was a poo-brown Datsun. Sid was skinnier than a rattlesnake he was half a person wide but he was double somebody to me. Sid was my dad *and* he was my mum and Healy stole him away so don't you dare talk to me about daylight robbery.

—

The thing you need to know about the Keres is: they didn't start it. Not ever. No it wasn't their fault. They'd fly down in flocks in fleets *in corps*. Featherlight but bonestrong. They'd blaze down like osprey like ravens like night yeah those Keres would finish things off.

—

I got pretty low after Sid went away you would too if your dad went down don't kid yourself you know you would.

He and Chook were sent to Silverwater Prison in Sydney it was only an hour or so by car but I wasn't old enough to drive and anyway Chook's Sandman had been impounded and who knows where the Sunbird was by now and sure I could catch a train and then get a bus but it's hardly the same as having Sid right there yeah they may as well of been jettisoned to the moon.

Don't get me wrong my dad was useless I told him so enough times it's just that without Sid there being hopeless *with me* I couldn't see the point of anything.

Our house knew it too. It gave way slowly at first and then in a rush of surrender leaking seeping peeling yielding. Snake vines grew through the besser-block letterbox their tendrils spilling out onto the drive their flowers smelling of mothballs smelling of rot. Sometime during Sid's court case the garden gnome had gone and got itself decapitated so now it sat by the empty pond and fished headlessly its hook snagged in the weeds that pushed up through cracks in the concrete. In the carport one corner of the PVC roof had lifted away from its jack-pipe pylon and it flapped in a panic whenever the wind picked up like a bird with a damaged wing. On the front door the three shiny barrel-bolt locks Sid had installed were already shedding their cheap paint it flaked off in bright burnished flecks like scales yeah it lay like gold dandruff on the porch.

Sid's stuff was still everywhere inside a metal drum slap bang in the middle of the lounge room while beside the TV a small fortress of boxed security locks sat gathering dust because there was no stock rotation. All those coils of wire and rolls of lino all those teetering stacks of car parts they all went undelivered because Sid and Chook weren't there to do it and no one ever came to collect them. I walked laps of that circuit like Sid used to do only slowly and less bouncy than Sid I scuffed along shuffled through that green shagpile carpet dragged myself from room to empty room. Then through the swing doors and into the kitchen a sawn-off piece of pipe sat on the benchtop. Thing was only short but as wide as a manhole cover Sid and Chook must've had plans for that pipe and now it sat on the kitchen bench like some sort of supersized egg ring it was too heavy to move I didn't have the heart to anyway.

In Sid's bedroom that one wardrobe door was still unhinged he never fixed it since the pig-eyed debt collector came visiting that day and it hung at a drunken angle half resting against the wall it was the top hinge that had been ripped clean off. At least the old man had bothered to flip his mattress so I didn't have to look at the slash marks the pig-eyed man had made. Sid had flipped it straight after it happened so the sliced side was facedown its leaking guts held in by the bed base.

After Sid went to prison I'd gone around the backyard unpegging dried-out tongues of biltong that flapped dolefully on the rusted wires of the clothesline those were the strips that had been rejected even by the kookaburras. I yanked them off and put them in the concrete trough in the back corner of the yard that Sid used to clean and gut fish I chucked that biltong in pegs and all. Then I set fire to it I watched it go up in flames.

It smelled bad as it burned dried meat and plastic pegs but I watched until it was ashes until it fizzled to nothing it was the end of Sid's biltong empire throw that one on the funeral pyre of lost dreams.

—

Technically I didn't need my own money technically Stevie's mum Mrs Madigan was my *kinship carer* which meant I had a room at Stevie's place and three meals a day and more brothers than you could poke a stick at yeah brothers wrestling in the corridor and playing keepy-uppy using the couch cushions and stinking out the bathroom worst of all.

Yeah Mrs Madigan put up her hand to be my carer I guess with three boys Mrs Madigan was short on sisterhood. Maybe that's why she'd been on at me since the beginning of time to call her Lorraine not Mrs Madigan. She'd said it that day when I'd dragged Stevie out of the bay and then she'd said it again just about every time I'd seen her since then.

Call Me Lorraine was what I called her when it was just me and Stevie on our own.

—

Call Me Lorraine was my temporary legal guardian at least until Sid was released from prison or until I turned eighteen whichever thing went and happened first. But given both of those things were still years away especially if Sid didn't behave himself then it didn't take a genius to see Mrs Madigan had signed up for the long haul seriously what a force of nature.

—

Still a girl's got to be financially independent yeah a room of one's own *and* some cash to stash in it. And so there I was back at Jabiru Avenue rooting around in Sid's sock drawer searching for money I emptied the drawer and checked in his socks Sid only owned three pairs and none of them matching but none of them full of cash either. I checked his fishing-tackle boxes gathering dust under the bed turned stained pillowcases inside out and ran my fingers along cracks in the vinyl lining of the wardrobe anywhere Sid might've hidden a wad of cash but the old man'd left nothing not a cent still no surprises there no wasn't really a newsflash to me. All Sid's money had been safely deposited down at Saratoga Racecourse that was my guess.

I'd given up on finding anything and was shoving Sid's fishing-tackle box back under the bed when my hand brushed against something it was hard but gently pebbled. I fumbled around oh it was his violin all musty and mute under there.

I sat back then and slid the case out with one toe the thing was machinegun shaped with Mendini inscribed on the handle and I didn't need to flip the metal clips and crack the lid to know what it looked like inside. Yeah I could picture its curves its f-holes curling like the flicks of a pen the polished maple of its back its belly the smooth worn feel of its neck.

That was it I could sell Sid's Mendini I could take it to Cash Converters on Mann Street that afternoon. I'd trade it in and put enough money in my pocket to buy a one-way bus ticket to Sydney. Then I'd find somewhere to stay somewhere near the prison so I could visit Sid I'd also see Chook. Silverwater Prison allowed two one-hour visits each week so I could drop by biweekly yeah drop in for a box visit and see Sid through a sheet of polycarbonate shoot the breeze through a sheet of Silverwater's best bulletproof perspex.

Who knows maybe they'd get to know me there at the prison guards' desk start to recognise me as Sid's kid. They might learn my name or slip me a couple of coins for the can machine yeah let me skip the drug search on some days.

All I had to do was sell Sid's violin what use was his fiddle to me anyway I was hardly going to whip out a waltz.

So why was I suddenly snivelling like Sid did when faced with a bucket of live bait oh I was soft as Sid trying to thread a warm prawn on a hook. I was bawling tears barrelling down both of my cheeks and my knees buckling my palms pressed to the floor and my face pressed against the cardboard case of Sid's Mendini breathing in its earthy smell.

Smell of rosin smell of pine smell of underbed scent. Soft smells. It was the smell of soft Sid.

So I shoved that violin back under the bed because I couldn't sell it hell I couldn't even lift up the lid.

—

Life got pretty normal for a while there living with Call Me Lorraine and Stevie and the rest of the Madigan boys yeah going to school and a piece of fruit alongside my sandwich in a hand-me-down A-Team lunchbox and the fact I had a lunchbox at all and the TV turned off during tea time and what time will you do your homework and all that jazz. Don't get me wrong I appreciated it I appreciated it heaps but there's only so much unadulterated kindness a person could hack like drinking cordial neat from the bottle also what might've been considered normal for the Madigans wasn't exactly day-to-day by my and Sid's standards.

For a start all their cups matched it might not seem like much but after you've spent your whole life drinking out of a McDonald's Happy Meal cup with scratchy Smurfs dancing around the rim or a tin camping mug or a plastic Pac-Man Slurpee cup or Sid's Reschs Dinner Ale mug he souvenired from the White Hart or a brown glazed coffee mug in the shape of an owl it was weird to be drinking out of a matching set of aluminium tumblers that came in all colours of the anodised rainbow.

There were other things too little things the kind of things that shouldn't matter but did like the way Call Me Lorraine expected us home by a certain time even though she'd already made us tell her where we were going. Or the way she liked to be in charge of how the groceries got put in the fridge. Or the way she bought groceries to put in the fridge at all. Or the way Stevie and his brothers couldn't squeeze the water out of a sponge at the kitchen sink after they'd used it but they could empty a carton of milk in a single go and then put it back in the fridge door for someone else. Or the way they could use three different bath towels getting dry after one shower. Or the way any one of them could eat a loaf of Tip Top just sitting there watching cartoons and ripping off the crusts and dangling them into their mouth and then balling up the soft centre until it took on the imprint of their fingers and then slam-dunking that dough ball into their mouth whole until they got through the entire loaf that way and then standing up with the sagging skin of plastic bag in one hand and the bread tie in the other and then wandering into the kitchen to ask Call Me Lorraine what was for dinner Jesus it made Sid and the Yattalunga B Division Rovers look lightweight by comparison.

But then Call Me Lorraine would go and make apricot chicken using real apricot nectar plus Maggi French-onion soup mix and you've never tasted anything like it. Call Me Lorraine always served me first on apricot-chicken night yeah before Stevie's brothers could get in. Plus then she'd keep some in reserve to put on our school sandwiches the next day when the sauce would go cold and syrupy yeah it was sickly sweet.

Chicken Kick-ons Stevie and I called the leftovers. Chicken Kick-on sandwiches.

So yeah some days at Stevie's house were alright you know. But some days I was blazing inside. Couldn't sleep couldn't think couldn't keep my bum in my seat I was churning I was raging. Ruby Red.

But even on those days on the afternoons when I would of put a gun to my temple rather than sit through another episode of *Family Feud* on the rumpus-room TV with Call Me Lorraine sipping shandies and playing along from her reclining chair yeah even on those days it was only ever my own brains I'd blow out and never anyone else's you know.

—

I spoke to Sid a bit when I was staying with Stevie's family. Spoke to him in jail. Spoke to him in six-minute slots. Timed phone calls before school was all that I got windows of time no wider than a letterbox slot.

But they were the rules the prison's rules not Call Me Lorraine's yeah she might've told Stevie's brothers no shoes on the couch and no wet towels on the floor and no milky cereal bowls shoved under beds and no sex under my roof but she wasn't a monster no she never did anything to get between Sid and me in fact she took me to visit him when she could even closed the bookshop just to do it.

Call Me Lorraine had to come with me too because unaccompanied minors were banned from New South Wales prisons that's right you've got to hold the hand of a responsible adult when you're visiting prison our justice system's rated R 18+. Which seems about right when you stop to think about it yeah the way we dole out justice in this country isn't suitable for children just ask all them kids in custody.

So Call Me Lorraine would take me down to Sydney to see Sid and she'd walk inside with me her sloppy red sandals squeaking on the lino her bare arms resting on the laminate at the front desk while she talked with the prison guards got the lowdown on the security arrangements for that day got a locker for us to put our stuff in because even though I never have anything with me Call Me Lorraine carted around a handbag the size of a small Pacific island containing wads of Kleenex tissues and crinkly bags of eucalyptus drops and reading glasses to go with her spare reading glasses and who knows whatever the hell else. And after that we'd file past the glass sliding door and troop up the corridor and some chick in a blue security uniform would pat us down and look inside our pockets inside our mouths touch our armpits run her hands up our t-shirts hold up our shoes check inside my thin white ankle socks and what a palaver just to see Sid's sad mug. And after that Sid would shuffle out and sit down. White overalls zip ties. His eyes heavy-lidded and slow.

And some days he was angry and some days he was remorseful and some days he was flipping monosyllabic.

Once we went to visit he was high as a kite oh Sid was buzzing alright. He'd started a ticket and he had runners in every block of the nine-block compound.

Betting on what I said.

This and that he replied.

A bloke could run a book on anything he said they'd take wagers on the cryptic ■ing crossword.

Another time when we arrived Sid was a no-show. The zombies at the front desk said he'd been transferred to another prison no he had a headache yeah he was in sickbay. Bit of a difference you want to try getting your story straight we said yeah corroborate your lies at least will you.

But what did they care they hadn't driven for more than an hour along the freeway in Call Me Lorraine's plucky Barina sticking to the left lane the entire time. They hadn't shut up the bookshop for the morning they hadn't packed Chicken Kick-on sandwiches for the car. It didn't matter what Call Me Lorraine explained while she pushed her red frames patiently up her nose. No it made no difference they refused to let us through to see Sid seriously what is it with this country and separating kids from their parents we've got form here oh we've got history.

In the end we gave up and we walked back outside and crossed the car park to where the Barina was quietly combusting in the midday sun and where some ■ had smashed the front passenger window they'd nicked fifty bucks out of the glove box and even Call Me Lorraine got pissy then.

—

This one time when we were driving home along the freeway Call Me Lorraine started asking about my plans and my future and stuff and I didn't know what to say I felt dumb even suggesting maybe I wanted to go to uni even though I hadn't stopped thinking about it since that time Sid said it in front of my class.

I needed Sid there in his Kiss the Chef apron.

—

There's a sentence I never thought I'd say.

—

Another time on the drive home from prison Call Me Lorraine asked had I ever thought about seeing a careers counsellor.

I told her we'd had one come into school last year and that he'd said: Tell me what you want to be and I'll tell you how to do it. And so I'd said a millionaire and he'd laughed in my face and said if he knew the answer to that then he wouldn't be a careers counsellor would he.

And out the window it was all freeway barricades and grey light poles it was the same landscape I saw out the Datsun window that first time we drove Sid's car home from the dealership only this time we were travelling north and the freeway was unfurling in reverse and also at half the speed.

—

Once I told Call Me Lorraine I thought *I* might be a counsellor but not the careers kind I don't know what made me say it.

I think I was just sick of feeling like a charity case you try being permanently pitied.

A counsellor she said. That's interesting why do you think you might like to do that what sort of counsellor do you want to be.

Here we go I thought.

We were in the car again and in the footwell there was a stack of dog-eared books: *Parent Awareness The Birth Order Book Why You Are the Way You Are Raising Positive Kids in a Negative World* by Zig Ziglar was that even a name. I rested my sneakers on the stack.

I guess I just like the idea of helping people who aren't so lucky as me I said.

And Call Me Lorraine tried to arrange her face in a way that didn't say: we just visited your only parent in prison.

Anyway do you want these I said.

There was a bag of Cheetos Cheese & Bacon Balls in the centre console and I opened them without waiting for an answer and I started to eat them noisily. Call Me Lorraine's ashtray was full of Sweet and Low sachets. Them and weight-loss chewing-gum wrappers.

You'd have to study hard to become a counsellor said Call Me Lorraine and she looked pointedly at me when she said it. You're capable of it you know.

I ate Cheetos and licked my orange fingers.

So she said again: You are. You're capable of doing well I hope your teachers have told you that.

And I said: Do you reckon these have real bacon in them and I held up the bag of Cheese & Bacon Balls.

And she started talking about Doctor Spock or someone and his ten hats of empowerment or some s█t like that and how I shouldn't wear the black hat of negativity all the time.

And I said I wasn't but that surely even she was sceptical about how much actual pork Cheetos put in their balls.

—

Honestly I don't know what was wrong with me I should've just said I wanted to be a marine biologist like every other girl at school.

—

You were so wild as a kid a real wildie Sid would tell me when I went to visit him in prison as if I was no longer a kid and like I was no longer wild.

You used to climb fences climb trees climb anything that wasn't nailed down he said. Do you remember when the council built that brand-new safety fence around Gosford Municipal Pool that thing was what three four five metres high and all safety glass and smooth bevelled edges and yet you scaled it before they could even cut the ribbon before they could officially open the thing.

Do you remember he said and he laughed.

You climbed that fence so fast that when you reached the top you paused for a moment sat there teetering on that lip of safety glass like you'd even surprised yourself. Then you shimmied down the other side and swaggered across the pool deck on the wrong side of the safety fence your yellow floaties so bright like they'd ignited in the morning sunshine and a look on your face then like you always knew you had it in you. You must've only been two or three years old he said.

Long time ago now I said.

—

I remember that day but. Remember sitting on that fence like sitting in mid-air yeah floating I was flipping levitating. Balanced on that safety glass I must've looked like I was held up by nothing but like everything else that was just a trick of the eye.

—

Once the dentist said I might need braces when I'm older yeah to fix that gap in my two front teeth. Sid laughed and said good luck putting fences on *her* teeth ha she's never seen one she can't scale. What he didn't say was: good luck getting that kind of money out of us because that much was obvious yeah that was no trick of the eye.

—

This one time Sid superglued his hand to a lump of wood. He'd been trying to fix something or other and I'd walked in on him in a panic rip it off rip it off me he'd yelped and when I couldn't do it didn't have the stomach to tear his palm clean off his hand then Sid swore and said that's why women are the weaker sex so I said: Wasn't me who glued myself to a lump of four-by-two.

Seriously sometimes Sid made me so mad I felt like I could f█ing levitate.

—

The thing you need to know about the Keres is that they didn't start it but they sure as hell finished things off.

—

I'll finish things off.

—

One afternoon after visiting Sid in prison I was out with Stevie and we bumped into Pook and Ferret from Yattalunga Cricket Club B Division Rovers. We were walking along the side of the main road when it happened Stevie was talking sh█ like always.

You know the mudflats behind the jetty can turn to quicksand if the tide is right he said.

You know I saw an eagle kill a possum on this road once.

You know they shoot possums in New Zealand.

You know they shoot squirrels in the States.

But then we saw Pook and Ferret drive past in Ferret's clapped-out bottle-green Kombi and I was saved from Stevie's wisdom they pulled over into the gravel on the side of the road and waited while I legged it over to Pook's passenger-side window.

Want a lift? Pook looked pleased to see me. Where're you headed jump in Stevie we'll drive you too.

Nah it's okay we're not going anywhere me and Stevie are just out for a wander.

But it must be thirty-five degrees out there.

It's not too hot.

It's not cold I'll tell you that for free said Pook.

Then Ferret leaned over and asked how I was because I hadn't seen them since Sid's day in court. They were all there that day all the B Division Rovers standing awkwardly out the front of the courthouse wearing brown-striped ties that someone must have got in a boxed set ten ties for I-don't-know how much but looking at them you sure hoped it was less than ten bucks.

Now though they were wearing faded red polo shirts that said Carl's Autos on the top pocket.

Youse have got work then I said.

We're getting by.

Ferret looked almost apologetic for saying so.

That's good I told him.

How's your old man.

Not getting out and about much I replied.

It was criminal what they did to him and Chook said Pook. Those bastards that did it should be the ones locked up yeah they should be the ones doing a collar and tie.

A what?

In my head I pictured those brown-striped ties of theirs. It must've been ten to a box because who'd sell nine ties. It was just that the Rovers only had nine necks to put them round and Chook and Sid they didn't need a tie. No they were decked out in their pea-green prison greens. Not that you would've got Sid in a tie anyway he'd rather put his neck in a noose.

A collar and tie Pook said. It means five years inside.

Four I corrected. Four years non-parole.

A car whooshed past. The inside of Ferret's van smelled like smokes and unwashed shirts and something else that was painfully familiar.

Do you need anything Ferret asked me.

She's okay she's staying with me Stevie said. With my mum and my brothers.

Still if there's anything you need you just ask you hear me.

I'd never seen Ferret look so serious.

And maybe it was Sid that van smelled of yeah maybe it was eau de middle-aged man.

Tell Sid and Chook we asked after them okay. We've put the Cup on hold until they get out.

What the Kangol Cup I said.

Yeah your old man's got the trophy socked away somewhere at home so we've put the tournament on ice for a bit said Pook. Anyway it's not the same without Sidney and Chook can't have the Cup without Chooky's Kangols.

You mean that tin cup full of Chook's charcoaled undies is at our place somewhere! Seriously you blokes are so gross.

Pook grinned.

Settle down we're not asking you to drink from it.

We'll get it for you Stevie volunteered.

That's okay Ferret said and he held up his hand to decline.

And it was a respect thing you could tell yeah respect for Sid and Chook. Say what you want about those B Division boys they weren't pretty but they had honour.

But if I get it will you play the Cup again I asked. Before Chook and Sid get out I mean. They'd like that I reckon. Might give them a boost.

So that's why I went back home.

—

Jabiru Avenue and corellas diving and screeching at dusk. They fly in murmuration over the bay pink shimmer real glycerine slick. Yeah one instant they're white then they flicker pale grey their faces are blood red. Dark-eyed. Then they rattle overhead and they land in the trees and they bicker and screech they dangle upside down and they pick off the bark.

Make the leaves shake like a wet dog.

Halfway up the hill our weatherboard house sat swollen in the afternoon sun its fat slats soaked up the sunshine looked just about ready to bust. Across the street at number six Mr Anders was weeding his lawn I waved but he didn't look up just stayed hunched over his grass must've been highly technical work that weeding yeah requiring complete concentration.

Up on the pink porch I found our front door jimmied open the wood busted and splintering near the knob all those barrel-bolt locks Sid had installed so carefully lying sliced like breadsticks like wafers. And I turned and looked over my shoulder but the yard was empty. Field of wheat-coloured weeds.

Hope you left it cleaner than you found it I said loudly and I toed the door open with my shoe.

The hallway. Green shagpile carpet and shadow-heavy walls. The smell of stale air and mouse pee. Also the spicy smell of biltong lingering. And the smell of Sid like a swift kneecapping.

Yeah you could smell Sid almost see him swagger through those swing doors in his blue Stubbies and thongs his thick bushranger beard yeah wearing that holey t-shirt that read Mount Panorama 1976. A good year 1976 it was the year Sid went and married Mum. A good year he'd say with a smile and he'd tell me how 1976 was the year he bet on Van Der Hum to win the Melbourne Cup and how everyone thought he was mad but then the heavens had opened only minutes before the race and it had rained so much it caused the track to flood yeah rained so much the jockeys needed snorkels and how Van Der Hum the stayer yeah that little Kiwi ripper preferred swimming to running any day and so that horse had romped it home and because of him so did Sid.

And Mum had got *Hum* plus a little horse tattooed on her wrist that's how impressed with Sid's win she'd been. Least that was Sid's story. Said she was smitten with her lucky husband yeah thought she'd won the lottery.

There was no sign that whoever had broken into our house was still there yeah there was no sign of life. Down the hallway and through the saloon doors the kitchen was silent gold sunshine poured in through the windows the fridge was switched off at the wall. Then through the dining room and into the lounge room scattered cables and pipes spilled everywhere a stack of VCR tapes had toppled over and their black bodies fanned out on the floor. In Sid's room the wardrobe was still half unhinged the mattress skinned of sheets as usual. But something felt off someone'd been in here. *Sid's violin.* I dropped onto my stomach to check.

It was still there yeah still under the bed safe alongside Sid's fishing sinkers and porno magazines. I reached under the bed and swiped along the shagpile and that Mendini slid smoothly to me. The case was so warm with summer heat I half expected a pulse I ran the pad of my finger over the inscription then I wrapped my hand around the black plastic handle and was about to pick it up when I worked out what was missing: that piece of pipe that huge sawn-off piece of lead pipe the one that had been sitting on the kitchen bench. It was gone that thing was big as a manhole cover it must've taken two people to lift it.

I gave Sid's violin case a nudge with my foot it slid easily towards the bedroom door and I stepped over it and left it there and then I headed back into the kitchen to check for that pipe. I'd get the violin on my way out.

I was right it was missing there was a great whacking space on the bench where that sawn-off pipe used to be plus a long scratch on the laminate where it exited stage left. But who'd take it seemed like a heavy way to earn money to me come to think of it who put it there in the first place.

That thing only showed up after Sid and Chook had been arrested were some of their mates using Jabiru Avenue as a clearing house. Had those bundles of copper wires in a pile in the lounge room been here last time honestly in this mess it was hard to say.

I was thirsty by then but the water had been disconnected or so I discovered when I tried the kitchen tap all I got was the *duh-duh-duhding* shuddering of empty pipes I let it run in case something eventually dribbled out but nothing did and when I turned the tap off silence settled heavily.

That's how I never heard the front door open yeah that tap was how I missed his footsteps in the hall so the first sign I had that he was in the house was when the saloon doors to the kitchen swung open.

Those doors started somewhere below his crotch and honestly they barely threatened his chest. Yeah most of his chest and his shoulders his neck and smug mug all of it towered above Sid's silly swing doors he made the rungs look like balsa wood sticks. His face was impassive his eyes steely blue. And that slick hair combed over like always he smoothed it down yeah he fixed invisible strays as the saloon doors swung closed against his back.

Don't let the door hit you on the way out I said trying to hide my shock.

And that got a smile from Sergeant Healy.

That how you treat guests around here what didn't Sidney teach you any manners think I'll stay if you don't mind.

I do mind so ████ off I said.

Now don't be like that I'd hate to have to bring charges against you be a crying shame to have to arrest you again.

You never properly arrested me. Like you *wrongfully* arrested Sid.

Wrongfully arrested? he repeated. I'm not sure you're remembering correctly.

I remember it ■■ing right.

—

At that moment the front door opened and banged shut there were footsteps in the hallway and two police officers in uniform appeared one of them was Constable Stanley who was almost nice to me down at the police station that day the other officer I didn't recognise. And Healy stepped forward to let the two officers through the swing doors and into the kitchen with us Constable Stanley looked genuinely miserable to be there meanwhile the other officer had one hand ready on his holster I don't know what he was expecting but you can bet it wasn't a teenage girl.

No no you're definitely mistaken Healy was saying he rubbed his jaw. You're forgetting the part where I wrongfully arrested Fowler too.

He laughed then. The sound slithered the length of my spine then it sat in the pit of my guts.

What are you doing here.

He ignored my question. Instead he hooked his fingers through his belt loops in that way that he had he jiggled his pants casually. In his black slacks and white shirt he f■■ing-well gleamed his blond hair was shiny with Brylcreem. Here was the sort of hero who could afford to fill his tank when he stopped off to get petrol.

He walked past me through the kitchen to the dining room while his constables stayed in the kitchen then he sat in Sid's chair and cracked his neck he swung his shoes up and onto the table.

Vultures he said can bite through a bone the width of a lamb's femur can you imagine that the width of a femur.

But I couldn't imagine that I couldn't imagine anything not with Sergeant Healy's shiny shoes on the table where Sid's form guide should be.

They're scavengers he continued. They eat bone marrow and their stomach acids can digest it they feed it to their baby vultures too. The only problem is: how to get the bone marrow out? That's why they fly up and drop their prey from a great height they do it to shatter their bones.

—

In the kitchen with my back against the hard edge of the bench I wondered where this was going and why Sergeant Healy was sitting in Sid's seat talking about birds and busted bones.

Seagulls do the same thing he went on. They pick up oysters and they fly forty feet up then drop them onto asphalt to smash them open. They do it in the bloody car park there behind Ettalong Diggers it's like f■■■ing hand grenades raining down.

But here's where it gets interesting he said.

If you fly high enough to crack that oyster shell open or if you're a vulture smashing baby-goat skeletons to smithereens then how do you stop other birds from swooping in and stealing your dinner before you can get back down to the ground to retrieve it? What's to stop another vulture or an eagle or a f█ing feral cat I suppose how should I know I'm not f█ing David Attenborough but what's to stop one of them from coming along and taking the food off your f█ing plate? Stealing from one of their own? Do you know what we call cops who steal from other cops he said. Dead f█ing meat!

He answered his own question and then he laughed like it was the funniest thing he'd ever heard. And that unnamed officer relaxed his hand off his holster he and Constable Stanley stood at one end of the L-shaped kitchen while I stood at the other.

Those seagulls Healy said now they're a dirty bird. A real dirty bird. Leaving f█g oyster shells all over the car park glory be leaving their mess for someone else to clean up. Me I like tidy work he said.

He unhooked his ankles where they were crossed on the tabletop and he recrossed them with the other foot on top then he leaned back further in Sid's chair yeah made himself at home.

I like tidy work he said again. I don't like loose ends and I don't trust anyone else to clean up my mess properly they always f█k it up that's why we're here isn't that right gentlemen you can't leave it up to others to tidy up after you because *how do you know they won't cut your f█g grass!*

He roared this last part and kicked a tub of Sid's fishing sinkers off the table and onto the floor the tub split and lead sinkers spilled out they rolled in all directions and some were as big as a ten-cent coin while others were the smallest ball bearings.

Constable Stanley flinched.

This isn't a gardening club! This is the New South Wales Police Service! Sergeant Healy said. We do *not* go around mowing each other's grass no we stick to what's rightfully ours!

That's a bit rich I said to him then. When you're sitting in my f████g house.

—

But Sergeant Healy didn't even acknowledge I spoke it was like I wasn't even there instead he lowered his feet slowly off the dining-room table his shoes making a dull thud where they hit the floor. He kicked with contempt at the fishing sinkers scattered like confetti clearing a path with the side of his shoe.

And behind him on a shelf I spied the Kangol Cup it was sitting by an old coiled fanbelt.

The thing is Nancy Drew what are *you* doing here Healy said to me. Did you think you'd try to catch whoever's been visiting this dump did you think you'd catch them red-handed was that your plan? Did you find our little stash hidden there in the freezer did you think you'd solve the case by yourself?

But the look on my face told him all he needed to know.

I'd never opened the freezer in the whole time I'd been back there was no point the thing was disconnected. I had no idea what he was talking about and didn't Sergeant Healy know it.

She hasn't seen it! he hooted to his two mates. She doesn't have a clue what I'm talking about look at her Nancy Drew here hasn't seen a thing.

He stood up then and walked into the kitchen at first I thought he was headed for me and I reached one arm behind me and fumbled against the drawers the top drawer was shut with the cutlery inside but the next one down was open just enough that a kid could slip one skinny hand in.

Cash said Healy. Cold hard cash!

He opened the freezer door like he was a game-show host and I was the carry-over champ and there on the white rungs were bundles of bank notes bound with pink rubber bands they were crisp-stiff inside their sealed sandwich bags and they were stacked in straight-edged piles. He reached into the freezer and as he did I slid my hand into the drawer behind me but I never turned my back no I faced him the whole time I felt around gingerly for a knife.

There had to be one in there I felt something curved and metal it could've been an eggbeater maybe something else was thin and wooden and then further back among the dust and the mouse droppings was the sharp edge I was after it was the knife I never used the other time Healy was here yeah Sid's second-best boning knife.

—

In the doorway Constable Stanley and his mate stood silent yeah focused on their fearless leader. They watched as Sergeant Healy withdrew his arm from the freezer in his hand was a clear plastic bag which he unzipped he pulled out a wad of cash. And when he shut the freezer door and turned to face me he flicked one slick thumb across the notes like he was going to shuffle the deck yeah like he was ready to deal.

He offered me the bundle.

I don't take bribes I said.

Bribes bribes! Sergeant Healy was jubilant. Did you hear that boys she thinks I'm offering her a bribe no wucking furries *a bribe*! What we've got here sweetheart looks like blackmail to me oh from where I'm standing we can brick you right up. Daughter of a convicted criminal. Left to fend for yourself and caught with enough counterfeit dough in your freezer to run a █████ bakery oh enough dough to feed the five thousand.

He wafted those notes in front of my nose.

Doesn't look good even by your standards he said. You have to admit it's not looking rosy.

—

Behind me my right hand was out of the drawer the boning knife tight in my grip. It was small it was the black plastic-handled one that Sid used to gut flathead and bream. Healy placed the stack of unbound bank notes on the bench there must've been two hundred fifties in that pile.

Why don't you take them up to Doyalson RSL Club he said and run them through the pokies for us and clean them up a bit.

Like hell I said. And I knocked the stack over and bills fluttered to the floor drifting in ellipses to the lino.

Now don't be like that even an old dog like Sidney picked up some new tricks in the end you'll get the hang of it.

They wouldn't let me through the door at the RSL I said let alone play the pokie machines you should know that.

You'll find a way around that sunshine he said. Resourceful girl like you.

Screw you I'm not laundering your dirty money.

Well then we're going to charge you he said simply. Constable Stanley's just the man for the job he went on. Isn't that right Constable. He's the one that's going to do it and then when they ask him about finding you here with a freezer full of cash he's going to hold the line aren't you Constable. Because if you don't I'll have to file a little report with Internal Affairs and you know how much I'd hate to do that Constable you know I can't abide paperwork.

He leaned against the freezer door.

You want to stay in our barbeque set don't you Constable Stanley he said. Well then get out your notebook and get your little pen and hurry the ████ up and get started.

At the far end of the kitchen there beside the saloon doors Constable Stanley had the decency to look uncomfortable. His face was red his hands flat against his regulation serge trousers he looked like a kid caught daydreaming in class yeah he made for a reluctant executioner. And from where I stood I couldn't see any mark on his cheek no there was no scar no nothing at all. No sign that his face met a tub of fleur-de-lis fence spikes in this very house not so long ago.

You're not going to arrest me I said to Constable Stanley. I still gripped Sid's knife.

What you don't think he's got the balls said Healy.

Having balls has got nothing to do with it I said to him with disgust.

And Sergeant Healy slammed his fist down on the formica bench and the last of the bills fluttered to the floor.

Constable Stanley he barked. Pull your finger out of your ███hole and get over here and do your job didn't they teach you anything at that ███ing university didn't you learn anything in all those ███ing books you couldn't chew gum and walk at the same time do I have to do everything myself.

Sarge. Coming Sarge.

Yeah well so's Christmas get a █████ move on she's not going to charge herself.

Over by the saloon doors Constable Stanley looked grim I honestly thought he might let me off the hook but then I came hard up against that blue wall of theirs oh those pigs they're all in it together.

Constable Stanley got out his handcuffs and they glinted yeah they winked silverflash in the afternoon sun that kitchen was as sepia as a childhood photo yeah a real Kodak moment right there. Then *flickclickwhirr* he fumbled around officially for a bit yeah took his time readying to put them on me.

He rides you like a █████ bike I said under my breath.

But Constable Stanley never put those cuffs on me.

—

To Sergeant Healy I said: What's your problem with me?

With you? I don't have any problem with you he said you're not even a pain in the neck like your █████ father you're nothing you're less than nothing.

He turned away and walked back to the dining-room table booting a large fishing sinker with his toe as he went the thing zinged across the lino and ricocheted off the wall it stopped by that stack of phone books.

It's because of Pep isn't it I said to Healy's immaculate back. It's because of my pop all those years ago and how he got chosen by the school inspector to go to school in the city and how your dad missed out yeah he missed out fair and square but you Healys never got over it. That's what this is about isn't it you can't stand that you got beaten by a McCoy.

—

I never expected that would be the thing that got his attention but Sergeant Healy turned around his hand sat relaxed on his holster.

Say that again he said.

And for once he didn't sound menacing in fact if you didn't know better you'd think he was genuinely curious but I refused to believe he'd hadn't heard the story before.

You know. What's history nothing but being doomed to repeat the past I said as if his memory needed jogging. My pop knew the answer and your dad didn't and now here you are still paying us back for it.

Sergeant Healy looked at me and I was aware this was the first time he'd ever seen me I mean the first time he'd really properly taken me in. Before that he always spoke to the room in general even when he was talking to me.

Say that again he repeated. He was intrigued.

What you know it. Pep that's my pop yeah he knew the answer to the school inspector's question I said.

And did you ever wonder how your *Pep* got to be so smart?

Sergeant Healy was amused now I could feel my temper rising felt the familiar burn behind my eyes I was about to be the butt of a joke either that or learn something I didn't want to know.

Do you know how your Pep got so smart he said again. Did you ever stop to think how a grub like him could ever know enough to get himself sent to a good school when he and his little family had only just crawled out of wherever they came from? Did you ever think about that?

And I said actually yeah I did. I knew *exactly* how Pep came by the answer: he learned it at his old school before Wyoming. And when Pep explained that to the school inspector afterwards he went ahead and picked Pep anyway because it wasn't every day you came across a kid who recognised good teaching when he saw it yeah a rare thing to find someone of Pep's age who valued education.

And didn't Sergeant Healy laugh about that yeah he just about burst his spleen.

Your grandad's been telling you porky pies he said.

It's true I protested.

Oh it's a lie he assured me. A real whopper.

You go ask Sid.

Sid's been making up bedtime stories. Your Pep got that placement because he stole the answers to the test. Not that I give a rat's ar█e. All happened long before me.

Bullsh█.

Scout's honour he said mockingly but instead of putting his fingers in the air he held up his gun and he wafted it like a promise.

Your Pep arrived on that first day at school with no respect for the order of things Sergeant Healy said. That's what my old man told me.

—

And while I held Sid's spare boning knife against the inside of my wrist and while Constable Stanley stood on the other side of me not able to spy the knife but not handcuffing me either while all this went on Sergeant Healy told me how Pep had turned up on his first day at a new school and how he'd ruffled some feathers by disrespecting Healy Senior on the oval before class and how Healy Senior didn't appreciate being disrespected on the oval before class – not by Pep and not by anyone – and as a result Pep found himself walking into Healy Senior's fat fist.

Sounds about right I said. So far so plausible.

But that's not the meat and potatoes he said. No the thing is your Pep – and Sergeant Healy spat out the syllable now – he *cheated* to get back at my old man who was all set to win that placement until your Pep broke into the principal's office and stole the school inspector's notes before class and every time the school inspector asked a question that maggot knew the answer you McCoys have always been lowlifes he said.

You're wrong the placement was based just on one question I said.

What? No it wasn't Healy said. What question?

I already told you: why do we learn history. So we're not doomed to repeat the mistakes of the past but even as I quoted I started to feel stupid.

You think an entire high school scholarship was based on one question you're as █████ dopey as your dad. No Pep knew every answer the inspector general asked that day probably had his cheat sheet sitting there in his lap.

—

I felt all the air rush out of me then and blood roared in my ears and any smartarsed remark was knocked clean out of me too. It was true I thought it made too much sense to be a lie. My Pep lied and cheated and did Sid lie about it too?

Sid'd always been so proud of Pep. Real educated man Sid had always claimed. Said Pep had learned things down there in the city. Said he'd learned things and that the thing about learning was that no one could ever take that away from you and yet here was Sergeant Healy doing just that. We weren't educated we were just thieves and liars talk about being doomed to repeat the mistakes of the past.

—

Get out I told Sergeant Healy. Get out of my house and take your dirty money with you.

I think you're forgetting you're under arrest sunshine you're coming with us to the station.

████ you.

Mind your manners I'm a sergeant I deserve respect from a bottom-feeder like you.

A fish rots from the head down I said.

Very clever he said and he got up from the table and walked over and hit me in the side of the head.

And hurry up with those ■■■■■ cuffs he said to Constable Stanley. Do you need me to draw you a diagram.

So Constable Stanley lined up the cuffs again I waited for the dead weight the cold metal but before he could get the job done Sergeant Healy spoke and I jerked involuntarily and those cuffs missed my wrists by a mile.

—

You're as wretched as your mother that was what Sergeant Healy said.

And I swear the floor shuddered below me.

What did you say.

Oh that's right I knew your *mum*.

And the way he said it made it sound like a dirty word.

Not personally he went on. Not in a Biblical sense but plenty out there who did isn't that right boys! But I'm sure you've already heard all about her yeah I bet Sidney filled you right in.

I stood and waited.

He was propped up by one arm on the cracked kitchen island he stared into the middle distance like he was on a f■■■ing yacht.

Oh you'd cross to the other side of the street when you saw her coming he said just so's you didn't catch anything! Ah you blokes are too young to remember her aren't you but she was doling it out alright oh she was loose as clowns' ■■■■■

pockets. Still got to feed the habit somehow I guess what you didn't know your mum was a junkie?

He raised his face to the water-stained ceiling and he laughed like his head might fall off.

Oh yes it all makes sense now doesn't it! Son of a gun! You're the offspring of a █████ junkie! Sid always loved a stray. Yairs he was always taking pity on some animal or other always throwing back a fish that was too small oh he was a regular wildlife lover a real bleeding █████ heart that Sidney. Bet he saw your poor mum as another feral needing protecting. Shame he wasn't with me when she died.

What I said weakly.

Third of May 1977 he said. The day your mum died.

A sliver of ice sliced through my rage.

How do you know that.

Says so right here on my medal he said.

And he reached in his pocket and pulled out a wallet he flipped it open there was a medal inside. Its ribbon was red and on the underside something was darkly embroidered.

May third 1977 he recited. Commendation for Brave Conduct. One less junkie on the streets thanks to me he said. And who knows what would've happened if I hadn't showed up. What Sid didn't tell you that part either? No? He didn't tell you I arrived on the scene and I found your mum dying of an overdose in a warehouse by the old Mann Street Plaza. Didn't he tell you how I sat with your mum while she died just me and her all alone in that great big old warehouse just the two of us there and her holding my hand her with that stupid █████ pony tattoo.

My mum died of a haemorrhage when I was three weeks old I said.

Your mum died from a drug overdose. I should know I made the ambulance call —

Stop.

— If only the ambulance had got there sooner.

Please.

— Shame I didn't call them till after she'd died.

And that's when I stabbed him with Sid's second-best knife.

—

The newspapers said it was an unprovoked attack that a sergeant and two constables attended the property following reports of a disturbance the newspapers said he was a decorated officer that he had a commendation for bravery. They said I was a minor and my dad was in jail. Were sure to mention I had a junkie mum. The newspapers said the injured officer was unarmed that he wasn't carrying a snub-nose Smith & Wesson revolver. The newspapers said I had a firearm maybe two that I'd been seen earlier buying ammunition. The newspapers said I was known to police I was an addict I had a police record. One said I was out on the street when the cop car arrived no I was armed and waiting inside by the timber sash windows. I was acting alone I had backup I was part of an organised-crime syndicate no I was dating a member of the Comancheros bikie gang. They said I was unhinged I was a criminal mastermind the newspapers said and they said and they said and they said yeah they couldn't get enough of the story. Couldn't get enough but also couldn't get it right.

—

Have you heard the one about the funeral you know the one: an Englishman a Scotsman and an Irishman walk into a bar. And the barman says: When the time comes what do you want people to say at your funeral and the Irishman says when it's my funeral I want them to say: Hey look he's moving!

I stabbed a police officer and not just any officer I stabbed Sergeant Healy so welcome to my funeral and now see me moving yeah watch me getting away.

—

It was late afternoon when I'd first got to our place so by now the sky should've been turning its attention to sunset yeah it should've been shedding its skin. Pink to orange to red to purple yeah we were due the whole glorious shebang but instead the sky stayed stubbornly cornflower blue. Stubborn as the sergeant's icy eyes.

And there was no wind either it was the calm before the storm no the eye of the cyclone more like it. That was it: it was the eye of the cyclone in our old kitchen the eye of the flipping typhoon.

And that wasn't even the weirdest part no the strangest thing was those birds. There were hundreds of them galahs starlings magpies currawongs all agitated and noisy as all hell they weren't settling into the trees for the night not roosting like they should've been.

—

Sergeant Healy roared when I stabbed him those cool eyes wide in surprise. The knife pierced the webbing between his thumb and forefinger and he was pinned to the laminate like a butterfly to a board stuck with Sid's second-best boning knife.

He looked at me and for once he was speechless it was the first time I'd seen the sergeant lost for words. And it felt good taking something away from him for a change. Yeah as magic as Sid whisking off the tablecloth without spilling a drop of his beer that one day. Then I pulled the blade out from his giant hand because I wanted to know if it would have the same effect coming out as it did going in. And it did and he bellowed and slammed his good hand on the bench in pain and what's funnier is that the effect stayed the same for me oh my satisfaction didn't fade a skerrick in removing the knife I would've stuck it in again given the chance.

She stabbed me? he asked like he wasn't right there like he wasn't bleeding all over the bench.

███ me boys she stabbed me!

And the second time he said it he wasn't asking anymore no he wasn't looking for confirmation. Now he lunged towards me his good hand clutching his injured one his eyes wild his chest heaving. He staggered sideways and then steadied himself and with his white shirt and his white hair that helmet of blond hair he seemed to disappear into the whiteness of the fridge.

And as he staggered veering first towards the kitchen island and then back towards the fridge the walls seemed to sway alongside him yeah they shimmied like seaweed in a rip. Then things began to throw themselves off shelves off benches off the dusty tops of cupboards an empty biscuit tin a jar a transistor radio a curl of cables slopped loosely to the floor sound of metal sound of glass sound of plastic sound of wire yeah the crack *whumpwhumpwhump* of things breaking spilling rolling twisting. They hurled themselves onto the floor but the lino rose up to meet them anyway. It rose up and then slumped back down and then rose up again in a different place like a winged thing was beginning to flex under there.

And the only thought I could hold in my head was the image of Sid whipping a tablecloth out from under a can of beer and for one confused instant I thought Sid was here. Did Sid whip the floor out from underneath us did I make this happen by thinking about Sid?

What the hell – said the constable in the doorway whose name I didn't know and who I'd almost forgotten was even there.

And he reached for his gun as if it could explain why cockroach baits pickled onions tins of No Name spaghetti rained down from the sky yeah as if his holster contained the answers.

And Sergeant Healy spied his opportunity he lunged at me and grabbed me by the throat the fingers of his good hand and also the fingers of his bleeding hand both wrapped easily around my neck my windpipe closing my pulse punching uselessly against his palms. He pushed his face up close to mine and he slid his jaw from left to right and back again as if he was getting warmed up.

You won't need an ambulance don't you █████ worry he said.

And I couldn't help it I dropped the knife and it went skidding across the floor and it slid underneath the warm fridge.

He squeezed harder then my feet almost rising off the ground my vision exploding into white sparks until the whole world the whole universe of Sid's kitchen gyred in front of my eyes.

And outside I could hear galahs their nails-down-chalkboard screeching and over Healy's shoulder and out the window I could see them with their pink heads and those bloodshot eyes I could see them rising up in spirals circling and rising and rising again. I could see starlings too scissoring across the sky and above them pale pelicans turned to specks by their height rising higher and higher becoming pinpricks against the blue and my mind was cut loose with those birds.

—

They say that birds know yeah they can sense seismic shifts even when their little bird legs don't touch the ground. Just like pigs can smell fear and dogs can sense death. Like you learn to avoid certain cops.

Those birds rose in an ascending spiral yeah a mass act of self-preservation so that when the next tremor hit those birds they were safe high above us.

And it might not have been as strong as that earthquake a hundred clicks up the road in Newcastle that one time when it hit 5.6 on the Richter scale. But the earthquake right now was still strong enough that the walls rattled dust fell from the ceiling and a piece of plaster dislodged and landed on the floor and left electric wiring dangling through the hole and Sergeant Healy shifted his feet yeah he had to plant them wider to keep his balance but still his hands stayed wrapped round my neck.

He was so close I could see his pink scalp visible beneath the part in his shiny hair and feel his hot breath he said what would Sid say when he got wind of the news I'd turned up dead but in that instant it was as if the sandbar we were standing on collapsed under a wave and the world vanished into sand swirl swell.

—

The sound of cracking was the first thing to hit me closely followed by bits of ceiling.

It fell in a hunk like the clumps of wet sand I used to try to excavate with one hand at the beach that ceiling fell in one chunk and the plasterboard didn't split up until it collided against the kitchen table and then it splintered into pieces. I saw the cop without a name go down too collapsing under the weight of the world under the weight of Sid's mouldy kitchen ceiling. Behind him Constable Stanley braced against the wooden doorframe he wasn't silly first sign of trouble and he was straight for the door past his mate standing there in the kitchen. Now he held himself up there where the saloon doors were swinging like Yosemite Sam himself had just barged through yeah dynamite sticks and all.

And Sergeant Healy he was standing closer to the falling ceiling than I was so close it must've shaved the lint off the back of his shirt. Yeah it was a close shave even by the sergeant's meticulous standards yeah a smooth one even in his slick book.

A close call and enough to scare the hell out of him and his hands fell away from my neck all it took was the actual sky to fall in f██ing end of days before that dog loosened his grip.

—

I ran then shoving tripping stumbling pitching forward and crawling when I needed to. Scrabbling across rubble and sucking in air and the ceiling lay in cheap shards on the lino and debris fell from the hole like dead birds.

And when I got near the doorway I could see Constable Stanley propped up there against the doorframe one of Sid's swinging doors at his back. On the ground in front of him half buried in wreckage and plasterboard the cop without a name was unconscious his head was tipped back and his eyes were shut tight and his Smith & Wesson winked at me from its holster.

And I thought how Constable Stanley let me walk free from a police station and how my hands were uncuffed thanks to him but I wasn't about to throw myself on his mercy a third time.

No a cop is a cop is a cop.

So I slid that handgun out of its holster and wrapped both hands round the brown pebbled grips what you think I didn't know my way around a six-shot revolver I could use that thing if I had to but it didn't come to that Constable Stanley let me pass the fact that I was holding a gun having something to do with it.

I left him and the unconscious cop there in the doorway meanwhile Sergeant Healy was braying from the kitchen. He shouted about stabbed hands and useless pr██ constables and don't let me get away but that kitchen bent and twisted as a stubbed cigarette Sergeant Healy wasn't getting out in a hurry.

—

I was. I was already away I was through the saloon doors and down the dark corridor and heading for the front door when I spied Sid's Mendini lying there in the bedroom doorway it was more use to me than to Sergeant Healy I reasoned yeah I was betting he was no Beethoven.

So I swiped Sid's violin held it in my left hand in my right I still gripped that revolver. And as I ran Sid's violin case swung lightly from its handle oh I could already tell from its weight there was no fiddle inside.

—

On Jabiru Avenue signs of the earthquake were everywhere and nowhere at once. An ancient hibiscus bush lay uprooted its spindly papery feet in the air a chicken-wire fence had escaped its stake and unravelled a crack had opened up in the bitumen or was that always there. Neighbours wandered out of their weatherboard houses looking shaken in every sense they walked around their front yards inspecting the damage and swearing at cars cradling fallen tree branches and peering suspiciously at roof tiles that were hanging in there. They seemed to move in slow motion like they were wading through water while I blazed down the hill and past the angophora that grew in the road not even an earthquake could rattle that thing it would put the apocalypse to bed.

And while all that was going on yeah in the shock and the confusion and the dazed neighbours and the shaky voices from inside and the trembly aftershocks and the elated kids' squeals and the wary dog standing guard on the front porch yeah in among everything that was going on sense seemed to jump ship and nobody seemed to notice when I sprinted past that gun was cool in my hand.

—

At the bottom of the hill I hit the dead end and that's where I should've turned left yeah I should've sprinted alongside the belly of the bay. But I panicked and I ran to the Good Ship Progress sitting faithfully upside down on the sand and I lifted it up and I slipped underneath with my gun and Sid's violin case and the last thing I saw as I closed the lid was the bellicose sky yeah slice of pinks and magentas and purples and red I swear you've never seen so much red in a single sunset it was burning it was hotly obscene and after that only black as I closed the lid and I lay on the cold sand it was a stone-cold mistake to hide under there.

SO NOW YOU KNOW

Hero was a woman. The first Hero yeah she was a woman she was a female alright. Hero the priestess of the goddess Aphrodite. Hero who lived in a tower with water views of the Hellespont so she could watch her boy swim his laps. You know: *Hero-and-Leander* Hero. Playing-with-fire Hero. What you never read Keats or Donne or Byron or Marlowe never had those blokes tell you all about being a girl. Hero was a woman and don't you forget it Hero was a woman so now you know.

—

This is how it ended but then you already know that yeah you knew it from the very beginning. I'm the only sucker who was turning the pages still wondering how it might go.

—

This is how it ended: things unravelled fast.

—

Things unravelled fast too fast for me to stop them I was Hero halfway up Jabiru Avenue and looking out over the water and I watched them unravel and I couldn't stop a thing yeah Hero in the tower that's me.

—

Seriously just delete that last part I'm no hero who wants to be a hero what dead with a statue that's a bloke thing oh that's a bloke ambition for sure. I'd pick alive and kicking over that any day yeah give me longevity anonymity better than any cold statue.

Still things unravelled fast no there's no denying that but did you have to go and say what you did – did you have to go and call it a foregone conclusion.

Yeah did you have to call it fate like you did.

—

I'm no hero I put my pants on one leg at a time same as everyone else does.

—

Holed up under that dinghy I was cramped and I was cold but worst of all I was barely a two-minute slow jog from Jabiru Avenue and Sergeant Healy oh seriously a girl could spit further.

That first hour or so under there I could hear sirens and engines and muffled voices on the jetty at some point a two-way radio sparked to life the cops must've been parked there near the shaggy she-oaks Code 2 they kept saying yeah that's what I was Police Code 2 that means urgent don't wait to finish tying up your laces Code 2 means get there flipping fast.

And peering through the timber planks of the hull I could hear all this I could make out dark shapes moving around between the slits in the slats maybe it was the SES rescue clearing debris I don't know it was hopeless trying to figure it out like trying to decode the Bayeux tapestry from inside a tight letterbox.

And I swear to God they must've walked past my boat twenty times its blue bum poking conspicuously out of the sand. And me: bum up in surrender underneath. Because there was no way I could stand up and walk out of there without neon-signing myself.

Oh I'd just stabbed a cop I'd just stabbed Sergeant Healy oh there was no going back now. I was just a kid without a mum and not even a dad and I'd just stabbed a cop oh yes I had. And underneath me the sand was cold and hard and where it had just been damp at first now it felt wet with the sunset and my knees and palms were raw and my skin was covered in goosebumps trembling shivering shaking my spine pressed against the hard gutter that held the bilge water and one hand frantically stroking Sid's violin case and one leg banging uncontrollably against the mooring chain of the dinghy like a fire alarm going off.

—

Then the sun was sinking like a besser block off a wharf there's no way they'd find me now without searchlights plus a pack of sniffer dogs and not when they had an earthquake clean-up to contend with yeah I reckoned I had a bit longer under there in order to gather my thoughts.

And I might've been too handy to the scene of the crime but what kind of idiot would look for me there surely no one could be that stupid. At least I had that on my side.

So I stayed crouched on the sand under my boat as the sun set and I shivered and shivered and shook. Yeah watch out for that sun you gotta watch that sun if you take your eyes off it for a minute then it goes and sets on you that's right it sinks yeah watch out for that sun it's sinking now yeah now you see it and now you don't just like that knife isn't that right Sergeant now you see it and now you don't oh it's hidden right there in your hand watch out for that knife Sergeant it sinks it's sinking I'm sunk.

—

I knew I wouldn't sleep that night but somehow I got that wrong too. Even with the sirens in the distance and the sand twitchy with soldier crabs and the oyster leases all shadowy there in the shallows like graves oh it was insomnia waiting to happen yeah it gave a girl the creeps but I was so exhausted that somehow I slept anyway.

And I didn't wake up until the mooring chain started clinking someone was lifting up the side of my boat. Then sunshine gushed in and I was scrabbling on the sand backing uselessly away it was the cops.

No it wasn't. It wasn't the cops at all it was Stevie I could have kissed his skinny face instead I settled on punching his arm he scared the bejesus out of me don't you know can't a girl sleep in peace.

—

When Stevie arrived and saw me huddled under there he clocked the police revolver in my right hand and the violin case in my left.

Jesus what's in there Al Capone he said pointing.

And if this was a cartoon then a supersized X-ray of that violin case would pop up and an AK-47 would be nestled inside but this was no cartoon and I had no AK-47 hell I didn't even have a violin.

—

And even without knowing all the gory details Stevie could see I was in strife who sleeps on the beach with a revolver in their hand hell who sleeps anywhere with a gun.

How'd you know I was here do you know what I've done did the cops follow you are they here?

But Stevie said no he was acting alone.

Honestly who writes this kid's scripts.

—

Stevie and I legged it after that. True we were completely exposed down there on the sand but it was still early the sun was only just up and the illegal shellfishers were still packing away from last night and those fat f■■s in the New South Wales Police Service were still tucked up asleep yeah they were snoring their bent hearts out or at least we hoped that's where they were.

Stevie said the coast was pretty clear on his walk down here and that he didn't have to overpower any cops singlehandedly although he did disable a police car on Barrack Street to stop them tailing him and by that he meant he never came within spitting distance of another single living soul and so I should go with him now it was as safe as it would get and it wasn't like I had a better offer.

—

We sprinted away from the shoreline and to a clump of she-oaks shifty there by the roadside. Stevie carried the violin case while I stuck to the revolver it wasn't that I didn't trust Stevie with my life just that I wasn't looking for ways to test the friendship by handing Stevie a loaded gun to wave around when he wasn't safe to walk with sharp scissors.

In the shadows I gave Stevie the abbreviated version of events and then we had an animated discussion about what to do next Stevie wanted to go along the rocks to an abandoned boat shed around the point towards Yattalunga we both knew it would be empty. But call it bluster or more likely fear but I wanted to go further wanted to get out of town altogether and put some distance between me and Jabiru Avenue even if it meant blazing out of there on a bike what like Stevie's idea was any better and there were three or more bikes lying unchained there by the jetty just begging to be taken for a burn.

Yeah we could head in the opposite direction away from the pointy end of the peninsula and off towards the freeway and then hitch up the coast or go inland maybe plenty of space there for a person to disappear. But Stevie said it was suicide to show my face this morning even if that face was just a windblown blur biking past at speed my jowls loose as a dog's and my hair a dead giveaway and so we had this ridiculous stalemate and the two of us stood and had a quiet domestic there under the she-oaks while those trees shrugged above us and the sun danced on the bay and three pelicans glided in casual as seaplanes.

And we'd still be there now with Stevie being as rusted on as a politician on a kickback yeah you've never seen Stevie when he's being pigheaded and me even worse but don't tell him that yeah we'd still be standing there arguing if it wasn't for that van that sidled up there beside us.

Lovers' tiff? Ferret said his head sticking out the driver's side window.

It was Ferret and Pook from Yattalunga Cricket Club B Division Rovers and I'd never been so happy to see Ferret's clapped-out green Kombi never felt so relieved in my life.

Ferret I called.

And Stevie and I bolted out from under the trees and across the gravel and slid open the rear door of the van before Ferret had a chance to argue. It looked like Stevie and I were both wrong and the answer wasn't hiding in a boat shed or stealing a bike the answer lay as Sid never got sick of saying with the B Division Rovers.

Inside it smelled like ciggies and the ghost of Chiko rolls past and Ferret and Pook were wearing their faded red Carl's Autos shirts they looked like Pizza Hut delivery drivers but too old.

Go go go burn rubber Stevie said.

And I think he thought he was in a movie yeah it was alright for him.

You late for something? Pook asked Stevie as Ferret eased the van painstakingly into first gear honestly we seemed to trundle along at five clicks an hour we would've been better off on bikes.

No we're on the run! Stevie said. On the run from the law because Ruby stabbed Sergeant Healy with a knife! A kitchen knife. Bam! Right there in the hand!

Deadset said Pook flatly.

Because that's how used to Stevie's bull■ stories he was.

It's true Stevie protested.

You hear that Ferret we're harbouring fugitives Pook went on. Coupla regular criminal masterminds in the van with us right here they're doing a bolt they're doing a Harold Holt.

Yeah well we take all sorts said Ferret.

—

We left the bay behind and we rumbled up the hill we were in the street that ran parallel to Jabiru Avenue and I squatted in the rear footwell in case there were cops and Ferret and Pook didn't bat one eyelid between them.

How's yer dad Ferret said.

It was always his first question say what you will but respect ran deep in the B Division.

He's okay I said.

Even though truth be told I wasn't sure how Sid was hadn't spoken to him for two days now. Also that sound was back now that roaring noise the fire in my brain like hitting a metal sheet with a hammer. It hummed. *Van Der Hummed*. It made it hard to concentrate on what anyone was saying.

Bit of a shake yesterday Pook said. You kids feel the earthquake never thought I'd see another earthquake after the Newcastle one thought I ate too many beans for breakfast.

I've felt bigger earthquakes said Stevie nonchalantly. Bigger even than the Newcastle one.

What when you fart in the bath said Pook.

I actually have Stevie said.

Sorry said Pook I forgot you lived on the San Andreas fault line I forgot you lived in Ancient Pompeii.

That's a volcano Ferret said.

All the same to me said Pook and he twisted around in his seat to grin at us. All the same to me they all cause a little shake rattle 'n' roll isn't that right kids.

Sh█ a brick there's roadblocks everywhere this morning he said squinting at the back window. They were setting one up on the road into town and now look they're putting one there by the jetty what a palaver.

Earthquake prevention he told us and then he grinned. Gosford Council never was quick out of the gates except when it comes to collecting rate payments.

He swivelled round to face the front again patting his seatbelt sash flat against his red Carl's Auto shirt and resting his hands on his bare knees.

The main road blocked then? Stevie wanted to know.

Only heading south.

Where are you two off to? Ferret asked.

But we hadn't reached an agreement on that I still hoped we'd make it north to the highway or maybe my best bet was to head west to the mountains yeah there in the national park.

We've gotta take some things round to Woy Woy said Pook we could drop you in at Gosford on the way.

But that was the last place we wanted to be right in the middle of everything and close to Wyoming besides.

We'll go to Woy Woy with you I said.

Suit yourselves Pook said.

So we skirted around the five-fingered bay past Gosford past Point Clare and Tascott and Koolewong and out towards Woy Woy. And I stayed crouched down on the floor the whole time with my head against the battered door and the revolver tucked in my waistband and I thought back to that day when I first rode in the brown Datsun beside Sid riding high there – riding shotgun – and how far we'd fallen yeah what a tumble from grace as I sat scrunched up in a footwell.

From down there mostly all I saw was blue sky. Blue sky and also chain-link fence.

But then I could see overhead train wires and the crust of Blackwall Mountain in the distance and I knew we were in Woy Woy. We drove past Peninsula Plaza I could see the top of its red-and-white sign rising up. Past Payless Superbarn and Capt'n Bream seafoods past the bakery because I saw the billboard for Viscount cigarettes (*Satisfaction as big as our land*). Past Chambers Real Estate and Rabbit Photo and beyond that Chinese poplars cut sharp against the blue and above them power lines and empty sky.

Youse two want to jump out here in town? Pook asked. Ferret and I have some business to attend to out on the back road.

Carl's Autos not paying the bills? Stevie said pointing to Pook's branded top pocket.

Call it insurance said Pook. A little Plan B in case Carl's all comes to a halt they'll sack you as soon as look at you in that place.

Just drop us on the back road as well said Stevie.

What you got business there too said Pook grinning.

So Ferret swung the van away from the bay and we drove out of town with the mountains looming on our left and dust from the road billowing behind us and we rumbled along the empty road all dry scrub and stringy spindly peppermints and in the distance a cleared paddock and the backside of a shed but before we got too close Ferret pulled over to let us out.

Sure you're going to be okay out here? Ferret asked me directly.

I nodded.

You want a lift home later? he said.

And Pook smirked.

Much later he said. Because after we're finished out here Ferret and I are heading back into Woy Woy gunna pay our taxes at the TAB.

There a horse race on? I asked him.

Doggies today.

Don't lose it all at once.

—

We told Ferret and Pook we'd make our own way home which was true for Stevie at least he'd catch the bus back home to Call Me Lorraine she was probably defrosting apricot chicken as we spoke. And then we slid the door back and jumped down from the green van Stevie clutching Sid's violin case and me with a revolver in my shorts.

And that was the last time we'd see Pook and Ferret and the green Kombi not that anything bad happened to them don't worry it didn't. But also that was the last time I saw Stevie Madigan before he went and shopped me to the cops.

—

Where to now boss he said when it was just us in the middle of the dusty road.

Over Stevie's shoulder in the scrub there was the skeleton of a bike track that had been abandoned crumbling jumps and overgrown paths and dockweed swallowing tracks in the dirt. Overhead a sea eagle circled and then saw somewhere better to be and it took off and the sky was empty again.

And Stevie didn't like it when I told him to walk back into town and catch the bus back home on his own.

It's that or wait out the front of the TAB for Ferret and Pook I said.

But what'll you do you can't stay out here with nothing to eat and nothing to drink you need somewhere to sleep or else you'll die he said.

It was the middle of summer I was hardly going to catch pneumonia he was being dramatic what he didn't think I could fend for myself.

I could come back and deliver food and supplies to you.

Okay sure just leave them somewhere around near the bike track I'll find them I said.

But when.

Anytime. Just whenever.

How long will you stay out here he asked.

I dunno I haven't worked that out yet.

But why'd you wait until Ferret and Pook drove off to tell me you didn't need me he said.

Yeah nah sorry I said. I hadn't really thought it through. Can I have my violin case now?

And he swore and went to dump it at my feet but that was too aggressive for Stevie even when he was pissed off and so he placed it daintily in the dirt and then he shrugged his skinny shoulders and left.

But the way he stomped off I don't know why he was carrying on it was barely ten minutes' walk to Woy Woy and all of it was downhill.

—

I didn't need an entourage I could change a light bulb on my own. What haven't you heard those stupid jokes you know how many blondes does it take to change a light bulb █ that it only takes one lone redhead to hide out from the cops.

—

Back then I wasn't taking Stevie down with me.

—

It was scabby scrubby territory out there no man's land and no woman's either not private property but not the council's problem if anyone bothered to ask them about it. Banksias and pampas grass stretched to the sky plus lantana and oleander and skunk vine and hawkweeds with morning glory smothering the whole thing like jungle cover.

Alligator weeds snaked everywhere.

It wasn't the hottest part of the day yet but my scalp prickled and my throat was dry and I headed off the road and into the shade of the scrub I must've looked like a freak with my violin case tucked high under one armpit and my peg leg limp on the side with the gun. It was quiet there in the trees a single black currawong sat and stared at me with its yellow eyes it didn't sing it was too hot for that too hot for anything but shutting the hell up. Its feathers were fluffed up and dusty from where it had been rolling in the dirt having a dust bath and I wanted to wash it and make it glistening glossily wet yeah I wanted to bathe it to give it water to drink oh I never wanted water so bad.

—

I stumbled on past the bike track the undergrowth wasn't as thick as I'd first thought from up on the road not nearly as thick as I'd hoped. I walked perpendicular to the road but not so far that I lost sight of its bitumen it was so dry the trees would bribe a dog.

When I got to the point where I couldn't see the road anymore I let Sid's violin case slip out from under my arm and I dragged the revolver from the waistband of my shorts and I lay both things reverentially down in the dirt. I found a tree to climb and with a bit of height I could see that a fire trail had been cleared to my left and also I could make out the property that Pook and Ferret were headed for over to my right there seemed to be sheds or maybe machinery along the boundary line something metallic spangled in the sun.

I climbed down from my tree and picked up my stuff and walked on. Straight ahead the slope petered out and if Sid was there he'd bet money on there being water down the other side. The ground was dry and I was wary of eastern brown snakes them and red-bellied blacks. Above the sun was a bottle top gold and flared at the edges.

At the top of the slope I saw Sid was right: there was a creek in the gully. It was too hard to tell from that distance if it was drinkable or if it was filthy with run-off and pollution from the property up the road. Still it was that or walk into Woy Woy to find a bubbler and I didn't have the stomach for encountering cops that day not Woy Woy ones or Wyoming ones not any.

—

Down the slope it got cooler darker fishbone ferns pushed up from rock faces tea-trees had tea-stained the water. I expected gungy and scum-pocked but what I got was clear and fast moving I wasn't hanging around for a second invitation I plunged in clothes on and mouth wide open it was icy it was ecstasy.

That creek was sun-dappled shade-mottled a thousand dancing daubs of brown bronze tawny ochre amber all glittering like the duco of Sid's doomed Datsun tingling with sunshine and life. Alien insects skimmed the surface and dark things darted below. And your skin when you held your palm under the surface those tannins they turned you golden molten yes that's what this was it was liquefied fire this was swimming in fire and not water.

—

Hard to say how long I floated in that creek chin up arms spreadeagled to the sky I wasn't hauling myself out in a hurry yeah not like I had somewhere to be. But then when I did finally drag myself out t-shirt wringing shorts absorbing more flipping creek than they left behind that's when I slipped and sprawled and sent Sid's violin case flying and discovered it was full of cash.

Oh there was more money in that Mendini case than a kid could comprehend crisp paper notes all loose and practically weightless. Well lighter at least than a full-size violin I cried with relief when I saw it.

—

Makes you think though: we could've been living like kings all that time with the cash Sid had stashed in that case.

—

Makes you think though: what were Sid and Chook doing at the Berowra truck stop the day they got arrested yeah if Sid already had this much money.

—

I had a charge sheet as long as your arm assault of a police officer attempted murder of a police officer unauthorised possession of a firearm resisting arrest. No horse no saddle as Sid would say.

—

I had a charge sheet as long as your arm but now I had some cash I had the means to make it longer.

—

Food was the first priority I hadn't eaten since before the cops showed up the day before hadn't been hungry until I'd washed

Sergeant Healy's blood off in the creek and after that I was ravenous yeah I could've eaten Ronald McDonald and washed him down with the Hamburglar.

And so I hit the road back into town taking care to give the TAB a wide berth in case I saw Pook or Ferret or even Stevie waiting out the front. I snaked past the Woy Woy RSL it was going off like a frog in a sock actually going off like pension day at the pokie machines if you want to be accurate.

I stuck to the shady side of the street I was wary of cops. That and the fact that I was hardly camouflaged what with my hair I mean. The only time I stopped was to slide a folded-up fifty into one of those Guide Dog donation boxes out the front of Fosseys there now I knew what it was to be rich.

—

Inside Deepwater Plaza I made a beeline for the burger joint one with the lot and extra beetroot keep the change yeah I ate that thing on the spot.

After that I got a shopping trolley at Kmart and loaded it up without caring what it cost there's a first time for everything right. Fleecy jacket long pants spare socks insect repellent sunscreen antiseptic plastic BIC lighters. I went around the camping section and selected a sleeping bag ground sheet waterproof tarp waterbag Esky fishing knife and a pack to put it all in I got carried away after that and picked out a folding deck chair in deep purple then thought better of it and put it back but I kept the roll-up mattress it was self-inflating like sleeping on clouds inflated with the tears of angels yeah I could just see it now.

At the checkout I started panicking because I thought the woman at the till recognised me off the news or something I was feeling pretty paranoid but she only said the discounts on camping gear didn't apply to fishing knives just so you know. She said it in this bored flat voice and then she went back to scanning.

I went to the supermarket and got food too obviously dried food and powdered milk and cereal in those silly mini boxes. And bread and apples and carrots and orange juice I'm a sucker for orange juice any chance I ever get. I got other stuff just what I could carry I won't bore you with the details of it but you should know I bought a box of chocolate Billabongs there were eight ice-creams to a box but I didn't need to worry about how to keep them cold because I worked my way methodically through that box on the walk back to camp yeah I tore off each wrapper and ate all eight myself oh I was queen of the ██████ world.

—

That roll-up mattress deflated on the very first night cheap Kmart crap I slept on sandstone and silt for pillows.

—

One thing I didn't get in town was bullets to be honest I wasn't sure where to buy them let alone what kind I needed to get. But I'd checked the chamber of the revolver it was fully loaded I wasn't much of a shot but I figured I wouldn't miss Sergeant Healy that many times he wasn't exactly what you'd call small.

—

I never had ideas of busting Sid out of prison doesn't mean I didn't lose hours daydreaming about it yeah of carrying him out over my shoulder.

—

I don't dream much here but last night I had this one dream that freaked me right out I won't tell you because other people's dreams bore me sh█less. Actually I changed my mind I will tell you I dreamed I was a giant mouth yeah a mouth the size of the back of a bus.

But for all its size my mouth couldn't make a single sound. Then just when I thought nothing would ever come out I watched as fistfuls of black feathers fell out from between my teeth like crow feathers or currawong's I don't know. Or maybe I'd been chowing down on those Keres I used to read so much about yeah maybe I ate one of them.

—

You know I really believed in those stories when I first read them now it seemed that they made me choke.

—

The author Charles Lamb he'd know what I'm on about. When he was a kid he watched while his teacher knocked some kid's tooth out by throwing a copy of Homer (not the Simpson's kind) at his head.

True story you couldn't even make this stuff up I told you those Greek myths were hard to swallow.

—

I thought about Sid a lot while I was out the back of Woy Woy he probably would've loved it he would've banged on and on and on about the silence.

And then when the magpies and the koels started up yeah when those wattlebirds began chock-carocking at way-too-early-o'clock well Sid would've been in his flipping element he would've loved all that racket as well.

—

You just know it wouldn't have been long before Sid dreamed up some get-rich-quick scheme out there yeah a sandstone-trading racket maybe or selling encyclopaedias tree to tree.

—

Kate was her name yeah my mum's name was Kate. I don't think I ever told you that. Kate and Sidney yeah that's my parents.

Or: Steak 'n' Kidney as Sidney preferred.

—

Mum was always there with us Sid made sure of that. If we were posing for a photo he'd say take it again your mother blinked and if he cooked meatloaf he'd say he was only doing it to get in her good books.

Ask your mother was his standard answer for anything he didn't want to agree to.

It's the way your mother likes it he'd say whenever he walked in without his shirt on. Well where do you think you came from he'd say when I complained.

And when I was littler and he went to place a bet at the TAB he'd leave me in the car out the front with the windows wound down and a roll of Life Savers in my chubby fist. Don't tell your mother he'd say with a wink.

—

You know what's funny the last time I saw Call Me Lorraine before everything happened you know like before I ended up here I actually called her Lorraine and not Mrs Madigan.

Her face lit up like a flipping Christmas tree.

—

Seen in a certain light everything can feel like a sign. An earthquake. An eagle. A gun. Truth is it doesn't mean anything no nothing feels █████ fateful. There are no signs and wonders just dead or alive and if you're lucky you get more of the latter.

And every time I think about my green book now I feel a small sharp recoil in the pit of my belly. *The Golden Treasury of Greek Mythology* what a rip-off yeah what a rort that thing was. Oh yeah it's all Greek to me.

F█████ lot of good those Keres did me where's Nemesis and those f█████ scales of justice.

—

Day one: my revolver and I set out to map our surroundings and believe me it didn't take long. Southwest there was scrub scrub and more scrub plus the bike track and the fire trail and the creek. And it didn't take a genius to get your bearings because the back road ran parallel to the whole shebang.

Supplies were not too shabby at that stage but morale was nothing to write home about. We abandoned any plans to explore more that afternoon and instead we swam in the creek what it was hotter than a witch's teat out there.

—

Day two: we went northwest we followed the road but we did it ten metres or so into the scrub so that we were out of sight of any back-road drivers like Ferret and Pook and who knows who else might have been cruising past.

Two's company said Revolver.

Three's a punch-on I agreed.

Revolver and I we weren't feeling so sociable.

We chucked a right from the bike track and walked towards the property where the B Division boys had business. From up on the slope it'd looked like a farm I'd seen harvesting machinery or something else metallic yeah something was catching the sun but that day we saw spear grass and heat haze and dust and the occasional telegraph pole.

A road sign the colour of melted margarine said this was Wilga Road why did that name sound familiar. Then the spear grass parted and sunbeams streamed down and there in front of us through a collapsed chain-link fence were three thousand or more scrap-metal cars rust buckets sh█boxes the lot of them and all lined up bumper bar to bumper bar yeah arse cheek to arse cheek so packed in they were actually touching in places it was a car-wrecking yard out there on the back road Sid would have blown an actual gasket if he'd seen it.

There didn't seem to be anyone around no not much in the way of customer service so Revolver and I walked the back perimeter then stepped over the fence where it was flattest to the grass. It's not trespassing if there's no tress to pass if you catch my drift it's not break and enter where there's no break-in to begin with.

Ford Escort Ford Cortina Holden Monaro Holden Torana hard to say was that a Charger honestly Sid would flip his lid. We zigzagged through the wrecks some were unlocked some with no doors at all in the distance Mangrove Mountain loomed.

The yard was empty but it couldn't have been abandoned because Pook and Ferret had been meeting someone there maybe there was a house or an office or a shed or something on the far side from where I approached.

We traced the perimeter hidden in spear grass there was no need to high-noon myself. On the western side there was a corrugated-iron shed junked with cast-off car parts and broken machinery and blue plastic milk crates and Jesus Christ fresh manure and some rusty tools and glass offcuts and stuff. Next door there was another shed and this one held dusty ten-litre bottles of water and several thigh-high drums I took a wild guess and one sniff confirmed it was petrol or at least it used to be. The drums were empty but less than a minute spent in there and the whiff sent me wheeling to the door. Seriously that petrol stung the nostrils worse than the cow sh█ did next door.

And hear me when I say I was no thief I could've easily helped myself to ropes and tarps and tools from the other shed but I nicked nothing I had money and so Revolver and me we'd queue at Deepwater Plaza just like everyone else.

Outside the perimeter of the property was ringed with dark pine trees rammed as close together as the cars. The whole place had the feel of fish in a can or maybe matches stuffed in their box. We called it a day then yeah and beat a retreat the sun was like a cigarette lighter on the back of my neck.

—

Back at camp my water bag had sprung a █████ leak spilled its guts all three litres evaporated in the sun I should've borrowed a bottle of water when I had the chance.

—

Supplies were dwindling faster than expected. Time Revolver went on rations.

—

Revolver and I had come too far to turn back. Not literally I just said we'd walked back to camp didn't I. No I meant things were too far gone for me to turn myself in the cops would jail me or worse you know they would.

—

Wait I *knew* that I recognised the name Wilga Road. From the pig-eyed man yeah that debt collector. The Wilga Road scrap yard was Sergeant Healy's scrap yard of choice.

Speaking of: there's another face only a mum could love.

—

I could hear colours and taste memories. Release the camels send out the search party were those sand dunes I was entering the heart of darkness.

—

It's the boredom that gets you and no one warns you about that yeah it kills you slowly the waiting I spun my wheels for three days in total just hanging around keeping a low profile. Three days was like zero point zero zero something percent of my life that's how bored I was yeah I was doing maths for f███s sake.

—

There was a mopoke nearby that went all night long seriously that bird was taking the piss. With his deadpan two-tone *boo-book boo-book*. Just quietly: I knew I'd miss old mate when I was gone.

—

No sign of Stevie Wonder when I was out there. No food parcels left by the bike track like we'd arranged. The Madigan meals-on-wheels service wasn't what it was cracked up to be Stevie must've been busy and stuff.

Or more likely Lorraine was keeping him on a tight leash no wandering off anywhere. Not with earthquakes and police investigations not with girls wielding kitchen knives yeah little Stevie was staying home the most adventurous thing he was allowed to do was lick the wooden spoon when Lorraine made apricot chicken.

—

Hey Stevie Wonder do you remember that time we played Would You Rather yeah remember we argued about the best way to die.

You said you'd rather drown and I said wait this was supposed to be a hypothetical conversation and you didn't have to try to drown yourself in the bay that one time.

And you punched me in the arm and said I was never going to let you live that down was I.

And so I punched you back but harder and then you shoved me down the side of that sand dune. How did I feel about death by sand burial you asked and I climbed back up and tackled you and said no thanks not unless it was quicksand I'd only accept a quick death.

And you said suck eggs because I was getting slowsand and a slow death and you shoved me down the dune again and by then we were both laughing so hard we almost forgot about Would You Rather until I got to the top of the dune again and then you said you wouldn't watch me die yeah you'd skip that scene if I didn't mind.

—

Burning. My answer is burning yeah I'd choose burning over drowning every time.

—

Back then I hadn't shot anyone but I knew if I ever did it would be Sergeant Healy's name on the bullet. And I wouldn't miss you could tell him that from me.

I could hit him blindfolded with a bucket on my head.

—

But before you tally up the body count: stop and cross off the most important one. I wasn't responsible for killing my mum I could put down that burden at last. That's right my mum never died from complications from giving birth to me it was that ■■■ Healy that took her life.

—

Who in their wildest dreams would've seen it'd be Sergeant Healy who'd exonerate me.

—

Day three: the sun started it. It was high and hot by the time I woke up it must've been almost midday. High noon and I had business to attend to and just like everyone else my business was at the car-wrecking yard.

I wasn't going to take my revolver that day and then I changed my mind at the last minute that's a girl's prerogative. I slipped the gun into my waistband it was loaded that's a girl's prerogative too.

—

The road to the scrap yard was hot and dry and dust rose in lassoes round my sneakers. The birds were silent and the trees stood torpid and the air was yellow and thick. The only time I stopped was when a black cormorant stepped out of the scrub and stalked awkwardly across the road its wings half raised its neck bent forward that bird was meant for the air not the land it was out of its depth out of water.

I was walking to the wrecking yard to get evidence it was the first step to clearing the McCoy name. If Wilga Road was where the foreman sent Sid and Chook to offload all that copper and if Wilga Road was where the pig-faced man fitted in well then you can bet your nanna's pension that the cops were involved I just had to figure out how.

And if the cops were involved then I was guessing that eventually the good sergeant was implicated. Didn't *The Golden Treasury of Greek Mythology* teach me all roads lead to Rome and by Rome I mean ███ing Sergeant Healy. Then when I got proof watch me go public with it yeah see me broadcast it to the world get the *Central Coast Advocate* on speed dial yeah I'd phone 2GO radio faster than you could say entrenched police corruption faster than you could say hello police tribunal.

So that was the plan yeah that was the Play it Again Sam why else drag myself to the slaughter. Because that's what it felt like walking to the wrecking yard lucky I was so pigheaded.

—

At the southeast corner of the car-wrecking yard yeah there at long-on in B Division parlance I stepped through a gap in the chain-link fence and like magic a cop car appeared. It was a white sedan a VL Commodore maybe or else a Falcon XD it galloped up like it was headed towards Patonga but when I expected it to go fanging past it swung into the driveway of the wrecking yard at the very last minute.

A bike was strapped to the back of the car whacked on quickly with a stretchy bungee cord it made the patrol car look like a family wagon going on holiday it would've been funny if it wasn't Stevie's bike.

Yeah that BMX belonged to Stevie I'd know it anywhere and what's worse it was him sitting up in the car but with his head reclining against the head rest and his elbow cocked at the window he looked strangely comfortable from where I was squatting God knows what stories Stevie'd been spinning the cops to wind up with the chauffeur treatment.

The car roared down the drive and turned hard it pulled up out the front of a dirty fibro hut. An office by the looks of it and with the car's nose to me now I could see WY plastered across its bonnet: Wyoming Local Area Command.

—

But if that was the first shock then the second came in quick yeah Sergeant Healy got out of the driver's side. Jesus Christ I came for proof not for the big man himself I was hardly going to fit that bastard in a doggy bag yeah hardly going to ziplock him up for admissible evidence he must've been there for a car-rebirthing racket. Either that or maybe the copper price was hitting its stride and he was there to collect his dividends or maybe it was a shakedown yeah that's it extortion he was there for his dues he was the tax man a feral abacus.

Either way I was dead meat if he saw me. [illegible] me Sergeant Healy what were the odds.

—

He was decked out in his usual style: black slacks crisp white shirt his sleeves were rolled up jauntily to his elbows like he might work up a sweat signing documents in that hut or more likely cracking skulls. He was badgeless and hatless no way to tell he was a cop his right hand was bandaged: neat white unimpeachable. His hair was slicked over and it glistened in the glare who did he think he might impress at a wrecking yard. High above him an eagle circled Sergeant Healy said something to Stevie and then he patted the car.

A nameless officer got out of the passenger side I didn't recognise him couldn't pick him from one of his own police force line-ups but when Constable Stanley emerged from the back seat he was unmistakable why did Healy always insist on dragging him along.

The three of them went into the fibro office leaving Stevie unattended in the car. Weird way to treat someone under suspicion or under arrest or whatever it was Stevie was under.

And you could imagine what it was like in there – in the office I mean not the car. Plastic venetian blinds and a slow-whirring fan a nudie calendar hanging above the desk. Yeah I didn't need an appointment to know its insides just like I knew the guts of their meeting as well. Threats and extortion and violence as well you could write it yourself now I was sure yeah you'd seen the truth of New South Wales's mighty police force you knew the true colours of the Blues.

—

Now was as good a time as any for me to move I figured I had a few minutes before they came back to the car and I had better places to be than hanging out in a wrecking yard with Sergeant Healy yeah fingernails I'd rather rip out. But when I stood my legs were shaky from squatting and also from fear. Sweat prickled at the backs of my knees.

I had just straightened up hand on hip or more accurately hand on revolver when Sergeant Healy walked back out through the office door he stepped into the sun and he whistled when he saw me.

Well giddy up he said calmly.

—

I could have shot him then without trying but I was no murderer I'd shoot myself before I killed in cold blood.

No earthquakes today he taunted meaning I wasn't getting away from him that easily.

No floods no storms no tidal waves he reeled them off but I wasn't hanging around to hear. I bolted.

No fires he barked at my back as I ran. He made no attempt to follow me.

I ran into a field where wrecked cars were parked they were lined up in neat rows and ladders. So many bricked-up bombs and all of them laid out in an anal-retentive Healy-neat grid. I thought it was smart to head into a field and not towards the road I thought he'd struggle to follow me on foot yeah without his patrol car I thought he'd be hobbled you know kneecapped but all I did was make myself a fast target.

Cicadas shrieked or was it the roar inside my head whatever the sound was sickening I zigzagged and dummied each row looked the same those cars winking like coins in the gutter.

A shot rang out then and not from my hand the cops they were firing at me. Specifically Constable Stanley was shooting I could see his bad stance from here yeah his arms were outstretched and his back was arched see the way he rocked back on his heels with the shot. I hit the decks I flattened myself in wild oats and dirt I gripped my gun I didn't think I could use it.

Sergeant Healy sure was breaking in Constable Stanley to the true ways of the Force oh he was blooding him bad. He'd be owned by his boss forever if he shot me now and if he didn't he'd be owned just the same.

When the firing stopped I saw I had laid down in the weeds between a Kingswood and the chassis of God knows what that used to be maybe a Torana it was hard to tell. Wait it was a Charger yeah *Valiant* it read that logo was about the last part still standing I rubbed it for luck no for justice for *revenge* I would've souvenired it if I had just one pocket.

I was on borrowed time but. Constable Stanley and the other unnamed officer would be working their way through the wrecks already crouching low spreading out closing in. Hell Sergeant Healy might even get in on the action so long as he didn't have to work up a sweat yeah fat chance he'd get his hands dirty whether they were bandaged or not f██ it I knew I had to move.

Hunching inching if you thought I was petrified you don't know the half of it I was packing sh█ yeah I was packing death. I edged out from behind that Valiant and straight into Constable Stanley well straight into his sights at least he was standing twenty or so metres away and he had his gun trained on me. And the voice of God namely the voice of Sergeant Healy told him to blow my brains out right now so he pulled the trigger but my gun fired first and Constable Stanley just buckled why what would you've done.

I staggered. Pain from the recoil shot up my shoulder and my neck and my jaw and my ears rang I righted myself. And Constable Stanley's foot jerked like he might just stand up and then it stopped dead oh God he was dead.

Sergeant Healy appeared then and he was so sure of himself so certain I wouldn't shoot again that he walked over to Constable Stanley he bent over and inspected the body what did he expect he was dead. And even from this distance I could hear Sergeant Healy call Constable Stanley something unprintable.

—

I never meant to kill Constable Stanley like that. Never meant it didn't want it and wish that I could take it back I was scared it was just a reflex on my part.

Believe me when I say I was shattered.

No I was *cooked* according to Sergeant Healy yeah that's what he shouted at me. I was cooked yeah he had me on a cracker he said I didn't doubt it for a second.

And all around me metal chassis dazzled in the glare they were like cans in a factory and at the far end of the field I could see the line of dark pines that ringfenced the property and I made a run for them no shots popped behind me.

—

The thing you need to know about the Keres is they didn't start it. They might've been goddesses of violent death black fates agents of fury bloodthirsty women of battle but the Keres only feasted on the bloody remains when Death had already arrived.

And that's important that's my point they're only there to end things I never asked for any of this. I was just there to finish things off yeah how's that for destiny.

When Constable Stanley died so did any plans I might've had all of them gone in an instant any idea that I might go to uni or whatever gone in a hairsbreadth.

—

Under those pines in the shadow of the trees in the shadow of the mountain somehow the air was still hot as a breath on your neck. I sat – fell – landed in a mess of needles yeah pine spines they lay tangled and matted my gun was still warm.

I needed water needed help but neither thing was on the cards the cavalry wasn't coming just like there was nothing to drink. Sweat slunk down the back of my neck.

Checked my gun tapped my bullets still five chances left. I wasted nothing shooting Constable Stanley and the efficiency kills me.

To my left under a pine a dead bird lay in the dust its wings in flight but its body disembowelled. Above a mackerel sky and patchy clouds assembled rippling repeating scales on a skyward fish. Yeah fish in the sky and birds in the dirt the whole world was reversed oh I was turned inside out.

See I said to Sid as if he was there and not inside Silverwater Prison. They never heard us no they never listened did they in the distance a car engine revved. If Sergeant Healy was coming for me I was going to lay out the red carpet. I could see dust rise up in plumes the cops were driving around the outside perimeter of the wrecking yard what a joke I was the insider for once.

—

Killing Constable Stanley was a blink of an eye and in that blink everything I knew about myself was lost all the stories I told myself about myself fell away I was an entirely different animal oh I was something wild at the same time I was as ancient as dust.

—

In the distance I could see that police car approaching it had passed the first corner and was onto the straight and I wasn't waiting for a second invitation. I ran out from the pines and for a sickening instant I was exposed. I sprinted to the car yard and the first car I came to was a rusted Gemini it was wheel-less windowless hell doorless on one side but on the far side a door was hanging loose as a tooth. And I reefed that door off it wasn't heavy not that big and I half carried it half dragged it back to the pines I wasn't so stupid as to think I didn't need protection I wasn't as deluded as that.

—

The police car had rounded the closest corner now I could see its white roof bright as a bandage it made its way towards me unravelling.

By the time it got to my pines and caught sight of me it had driven past it swerved sharply and looped back bumping over grass tussocks Sid would've appreciated the manoeuvre. I crouched and watched as Sergeant Healy got out of the passenger side the unnamed cop he moved slower. In the back seat Stevie sat his head swivelling alert and I stood as Sergeant Healy walked towards me his gun was in its holster.

Take your hat off when you're talking to me he said. He pointed at my car-door armour.

I held it at hip height the bottom edge of the door stopped above my bare knees bronze duco protected my torso while the windowless frame it band-aided my nose metallic strip where a zinc stripe should be.

I ignored his instruction you could tell he was unfamiliar with that.

You people you have no respect that's the problem he said.

You people like there were more of me there in the dust and the glare yeah like each car door had someone crouched down behind it.

I stood stony still but the rubber door seal dangled ridiculously down my side.

You know how we found you here today Sergeant Healy said. And as he spoke he walked towards me behind him the other cop had him covered.

We found you he said again thanks to your mate Madigan that's right Steven here ratted you out.

Liar I said.

Liar? Sergeant Healy repeated. What you've never known Steven here to shoot his mouth off you've never known him to talk too much. No?

I looked over his shoulder at the Boy Who Cried Wolf sitting up in there in that cop car and I could see his traitorous head through the back window but both his Janus faces were obscured.

—

It was enough to make me put down that door I was holding I lowered its edge to the dirt. I'd had it with being let down and lied to and now I let that door fall to the ground the rubber seal snaked away in the grass. I had so much fury inside me I never knew how much the roar in my head was unbearable I was revenge I was war I was the Keres no I was that ruby-red scroll in the grip of the eagle I was Nemesis now watch me unfurl.

—

Don't let the door hit you on the way out isn't that what Sid always said.

—

But then there was an urgent banging on the inside of the police patrol car window and a sandwich bag rose like the sun. And a grease mark was visible it was Chicken Kick-on oh see Stevie never betrayed me to the cops no he was just bringing me lunch.

—

Wooheee Sergeant Healy hooted when he saw me standing there exposed my door lying face down in the dust. What a bobby dazzler boys!

He stopped walking towards me now yeah refused to step into the shade of the pines instead he stood legs apart in the sunlight his white shirt was dazzling pristine that was the most repulsive part and it was late afternoon when I reached for my gun the sky curling red at the edges. And I refused to be small to be shamed *to be Sid*.

You wouldn't he said right before I shot him.

—

I swear to you that's how it happened.

A NOTE ON SOURCES

Red contains several deliberate nods to Ned Kelly's Jerilderie Letter: Ned Kelly, *Letter, known as the Jerilderie Letter, in Joe Byrne's hand*, February 1879, manuscript, gift of Bronwyn Binns, 2000, State Library of Victoria.

Page references for the Jerilderie Letter are taken from National Museum Australia's transcript: www.nma.gov.au/explore/features/ned-kelly-jerilderie-letter/transcription

p. 1: 'I didn't know what a shotgun was wouldn't have known one if it bit me on the bum'

On page 22 of the Jerilderie Letter, Kelly writes: 'those two quiet hardworking innocent men who would not know the difference in a revolver and a saucepan handle'.

p. 121: 'Down there where the ground was so rotten it would bog a duck.'

On page 1, Kelly writes: 'The ground was that rotten it would bog a duck in places'.

p. 191: 'and as a result Pep found himself walking into Healy Senior's fat fist'

On page 4, Kelly writes: 'my fist came in collision with McCormack's nose'.

p. 229: 'No I meant things were too far gone for me to turn myself in'

On page 23, Kelly writes: 'knew I would get no justice if I gave myself up'.

p. 236: 'I could have shot him then without trying but I was no murderer I'd shoot myself before I killed in cold blood.'

On page 29, Kelly writes: 'I could have shot them without speaking but their lives was no good to me'.

p. 238: 'Sergeant Healy told him to blow my brains out'

On page 21, Kelly writes: 'The trooper pulled out his revolver and said he would blow her brains out if she interfered in the arrest.'

***Red* also references several other texts:**

p. 30: 'Your dad thinks he's John Wayne.'

A reference to the 1986 song 'John Wayne' by John Martyn.

p. 53: 'and the magpies cardle-wardelling'

A deliberate reference to Denis Glover's poem 'The Magpies', first published in his 1964 anthology *Enter Without Knocking*: 'and Quardle oodle ardle wardle doodle / The magpies said'.

p. 57: 'eyes sloeblack and wings crowblack'

A reference to the opening line of Dylan Thomas's 1954 radio play *Under Milk Wood*: 'the sloeblack, slow, black, crowblack, fishingboat-bobbing sea'.

p. 152: 'You see the cards you play the cards he said.'

Expression based on the title of the Coen brothers' short film 'You seen 'em, you play 'em' from their 2018 film *The Ballad of Buster Scruggs*.

p. 159: 'easy as a █████ Sunday morning'

A nod to the Lionel Richie/Commodores 1977 song 'Easy'.

p. 226: 'it was hotter than a witch's teat out there'

Deliberate misquote taken from J.D. Salinger's 1951 novel *A Catcher in the Rye*: 'Anyway, it was December and all, and it was cold as a witch's teat.'

p. 231: 'you said you wouldn't watch me die yeah you'd skip that scene if I didn't mind'

Deliberate misquote taken from the 1969 film *Butch Cassidy and the Sundance Kid*: 'I won't watch you die. I'll miss that scene if you don't mind.'

p. 234: 'a feral abacus'

Paul Keating famously referred to John Hewson as a 'feral abacus' in the lead-up to the 1993 federal election.

ACKNOWLEDGEMENTS

As always, I'm enormously grateful to my agent, Tara Wynne, and my publisher, Catherine Milne. Wonders, both.

Thank you to Caitlan Cooper-Trent and the rest of the family at Curtis Brown literary agency. Thank you HarperCollins and all who sail in her. In particular: Madeleine James, Alex Nahlous, Annabel Adair, Darren Holt, Lucy Inglis, Andrea Johnson and Hannah Jermyn. Thank you Meg Hoult and the team at Bolinda audiobooks.

Heartfelt thanks to Brendan Cowell, Sacha Horler, Emma Ward, Jaclyn Prescott, James Cameron, Brooke and Ben McAlary, Rebecca Cregan, my friends at the Best Little Bookshop in Town, and everybody else who has listened to me bang on about my book.

All my gratitude to my family, especially Mum and Dad.

Most of all, thank you Andy, Daisy and Georgia.